PASSCHENDAELE

PASSCHENDAELE

THE NOVEL BASED ON THE SCREENPLAY BY PAUL GROSS

HarperCollins*Publishers*Ltd

Passchendaele
Novelization based on the screenplay by Paul Gross.
Copyright © 2008 by HarperCollins Publishers Ltd
All rights reserved.

Published by HarperCollins Publishers Ltd.

The publisher wishes to thank Dr. Tim Cook of the
Canadian War Museum for his kind assistance.

HarperCollins books may be purchased for educational,
business, or sales promotional use through our
Special Markets Department.

HarperCollins Publishers Ltd
2 Bloor Street East, 20th Floor
Toronto, Ontario, Canada
M4W 1A8

www.harpercollins.ca

Library and Archives Canada Cataloguing in Publication
information is available

ISBN 978-1-55468-290-4

Printed and bound in the United States
RRD 9 8 7 6 5 4 3 2 1

To *Michael Joseph Dunne*
Reg. #447977
C.E.F.

Turning and turning in the widening gyre
The falcon cannot hear the falconer;
Things fall apart; the centre cannot hold;
Mere anarchy is loosed upon the world,
The blood-dimmed tide is loosed, and everywhere
The ceremony of innocence is drowned;
The best lack all conviction, while the worst
Are full of passionate intensity.

Surely some revelation is at hand;
Surely the Second Coming is at hand.
The Second Coming! Hardly are those words out
When a vast image out of Spiritus Mundi
Troubles my sight: somewhere in sands of
   the desert
A shape with lion body and the head of a man,
A gaze blank and pitiless as the sun,
Is moving its slow thighs, while all about it
Reel shadows of the indignant desert birds.
The darkness drops again; but now I know
That twenty centuries of stony sleep
Were vexed to nightmare by a rocking cradle,
And what rough beast, its hour come round
   at last,
Slouches towards Bethlehem to be born?

—William Butler Yeats,
"The Second Coming"

PASSCHENDAELE

NEAR THE TOWN OF ARRAS

THE ENTIRE PLATOON came under attack near a tiny French town called Maroeuil; the planes flew in low and quick, though the drone of propellers served as a warning and sent everyone running. The RAF was nowhere in sight, and the Fokkers kept turning around and coming in, each time strafing all things living and inanimate, the air clogging with risen field mud and earth. This went on and on. With each assault, the platoon splintered a little further, until Dunne and a few of the soldiers in his command were separated from the rest of the Canadians. When the air finally cleared, they were alone and lost. They had no provisions other than canteens of water, and only the position of the sun to guide them.

There were just the four of them: Dunne, Skinner, Peters and the Sarcee Indian named Highway, whom Dunne knew from back home. Slowly, they marched out of a pasture and onto a road that, they hoped, might link up to the one leading to Arras. They looked in every direction and agreed to head northeast, more or less.

They began marching. From far off the men could hear the distant echo of artillery, though it was so faint they couldn't make out whether it was their own or the enemy's or both. They wore woollen uniforms and heavy, hobnailed boots, both of which caused them to sweat profusely. Gradually, hunger set in; Dunne's stomach gurgled and his legs became weak and he began to feel light-headed.

"What do we do?" asked Highway.

"Only thing we can do," said Dunne. "Keep going."

Every half-hour or so they reached a divergence of roadways; as they were well out in the country, signs were few and far between, and many had been torched by the Huns when they'd been through. At each junction, they had to guess which roadway would end up curving back toward the road leading to Arras. Sometimes they picked the

4

right road, sometimes they weren't sure, and other times they'd arrive back to the same junction after an hour or two of pointless meandering. It was during one of these unintentional detours that Peters suddenly yelled, "Look!"

Dunne saw it too: a grove filled with apple trees. They all ran toward it and started plucking apples, and then they sat and ate until their lips burned and their stomachs felt queasy. After packing their pockets with as many apples as they could carry, they set off again, following country lanes past farmland empty of pigs and sheep and cattle. It was a hot summer day, and they had to force themselves to drink as little as possible from their canteens. They passed few civilians, and the ones they did see looked blank-eyed and hollow. Whenever the men wanted, Dunne let them rest under the shade of an oak tree and smoke; these breaks didn't last long, for they all knew they needed to stumble upon a town, at which point they would be able to figure out where they were, and quite possibly find something substantial to eat. Around four o'clock, they rounded a long, slow bend in the road. They passed a set of ruined farmhouses and started along a laneway covered by a cathedral of tall, shady oaks. After a hundred yards, they saw a village sign reading *Pouloise*. Dunne pulled out his map and looked hard and finally said, "There it is."

"Are we near the road to Arras?" Highway asked.

"Not really," Dunne answered. "But at least we know where we are now."

They kept walking. When they reached the village square, the men stopped and took in the destruction. The youngest of the crew, Peters, said, "Ah, Christ."

"Yeah," said Dunne, for he had hoped to stumble across a town that had escaped the fighting. This was not such a place: the square was a patchwork of craters, the front of the *église* had been torn away and most of the buildings lining the square were missing either walls or roof or in some cases the foundation. Only after they'd surveyed the square for a minute or two did someone point to the far side of the square, at a vegetable store that seemed more or less intact.

"You think it's still open?" asked Highway.

"Probably not," said Dunne, and they started heading toward it, their heads lowered with trepidation. They were about fifty yards from the store when the first bomb erupted; the air rained rotting fruit and old potatoes and splintered wood and shards of broken glass. Fearing simultaneous fire, Dunne yelled, "Take cover!" and they all dove behind any barrier they could find. The second explosion came within moments of the first, again lighting the skies with a burnished silver flash. The air thickened with dust, swirling paper and tiny fragments of brick. There was yelling and the bitter reek of cordite mixed with decomposing flesh, and when Dunne looked up he could see that flames were shooting from the blown-out window of the store. His back was against the remains of an old stone fountain, and in the deafening confusion of the moment he could not remember either running or reaching its shelter. Beside him sat a headless corpse, its back also against the fountain, its legs kilted and splayed. Its stench was outrageous and vile, like something torn from hell.

Dunne whistled.

Through the cover of risen smoke, he saw Highway come running. Behind him was Skinner. Halfway across the ruined square they grabbed Peters, and when the three made it to the shelter of the pockmarked fountain Peters saw the headless British soldier and started muttering, "Oh Jesus, oh Jesus," and in his panic his head rose above the edge of the fountain. Dunne grabbed him and pulled him down and told him to stay the fuck that way.

Skinner eyed the corpse while covering his nose with his shirt.

"Jesus. Where's he from?"

"51st skirt," said Highway.

"I thought the Tommies were up round Hill Sixty."

"Must've lost his head."

There was grim, momentary laughter and then the four men went quiet. From across the square, they heard yelling in German, but soon these voices fell away and there was nothing but the sound of wind and the pitter-pat of debris settling on cobblestone. Dunne reached into the inside pocket of his jacket and produced a Lifeguard periscope. He extended it and peered over the edge of the fountain; he saw a dusty, sepia reflection of the church on the opposite end of the square. Through the blown-away front wall he spotted a machine-gun nest erected on the church's debris-strewn altar. Above the nest, a cross still hung from the roof of the nave by a length of chain. For a moment, Dunne watched, transfixed by the way the cross languidly revolved in the surrounding chaos.

There was a burst of machine-gun fire and the upper mirror of Dunne's periscope shattered above him. Small bits of glass landed on his helmet.

"They in there, sarge?" asked Skinner.

"Seem to be."

"Who the hell would put a gun nest in a church?" asked Highway.

"Up round Wipers they put one in a bar," said Skinner.

"What do we do?" asked Highway.

"We stay here and they'll chip away the fountain until there's nothing left," said Dunne.

"It's a possibility," said Highway.

Dunne wiped at the sweat dripping into his eyes and let his lungs fill with dusty air. He tasted the ammonia of rot on his lips and he spat it away. He hated the part of him that enjoyed not knowing whether they would survive this moment.

"Highway," he said. "You and Skinner work your way up that side. Peters, you come with me."

The others nodded.

"*Go.*"

The four soldiers sprang to their feet and charged to either side of the square, Dunne and Peters diving behind a low, ruined wall. Dunne looked over and saw Skinner reach the shelter of a fragmented foundation at the same moment the Huns in the church responded with machine-gun fire. Highway jerked and pulled up short and fell in a twisted crumple. Dunne took a Mills bomb from the back of Peters's pack and lobbed it at the church. In the ensuing rain of dust and pebble, he raced across the square and grabbed Highway by a strap on his pack and dragged him next to Skinner. Highway was trembling and sweating and grinding his yellow teeth, though it was Skinner who, for some reason, kept saying, "I'm okay, I'm okay, sarge, I'm okay."

Dunne ripped open a pack of field dressing and attended to the Indian.

"You're gonna be okay, Highway."

Highway didn't respond. But Skinner kept muttering, "I'm okay, I'm okay, just getting my breath ..."

"Yeah, you're fine, Skinner," said Dunne. "Now gimme your dressing. I need another."

"It's okay, it's okay," Skinner said yet again.

"Mikey," said Highway. "Sweet Jesus."

"Hang on, Highway."

"This is kind of funny," said Skinner.

"Just gimme your dressing."

"It's okay," Skinner said yet again, his voice odd and far-off and hollow. "It's just a little bit funny."

"For Christ's *sake*, Skinner!"

"It's okay, it's a little bit funny, kind of funny, okay ..."

Skinner's words then became incoherent mumblings. Dunne and Highway turned and for the first time noticed that Skinner had been hit and that blood was gurgling up through a chasm in his windpipe. As they watched, Skinner died kneeling, his eyes still open and fixed on the debris-cluttered street. Across the square, Dunne saw Peters start to rock back and forth, hugging himself.

Dunne looked at Highway, who was still shivering.

"We're a long way from the foothills," said the Indian.

"You're going to be okay," Dunne said as he wrestled with another dressing pack. "I'm going to get you out of here."

"What I wouldn't give to be back in Alberta, huh, Mikey?"

"You and me both."

"Do us a little riding, a little bronco busting. A little salooning. Like the old days."

"Like the old days."

"Maybe even look up Royster. Jesus Christ, we were a wild bunch."

"Still are. Now shut up."

"Promise me you'll get me outta here."

"I will."

"How you going to do that?"

"Just will."

Dunne looked around. He saw a horse, still attached to its harness, walking dazed and wounded through a smoky haze. He noticed an empty birdcage, its door bent and rusted and open, still hanging from the remains of a fallen building. There was something about the emptiness of the cage that exhausted the sergeant and made him feel as though he no longer cared about what happened to him or his men. He often had this feeling, and it was something that scared him more than enemy fire or booby-trapped roadways or gas. Dunne leaned his head against the crumbling wall and took a shallow breath. He had been at Vimy too, and he was bitter that they hadn't let him go home for good afterwards.

Fuck it, he thought. They want to kill me they can go ahead.

He pulled out a swath of white field dressing and tied it to the barrel of his rifle. He rose with his gun in the air, both his gradual movements and the flag tied to his weapon indicating surrender. He now saw there were four German gunners in the pulpit. They looked at one another.

"Fall in behind," Dunne called to Peters, who was still holding himself and rocking and muttering words of self-comfort.

Peters rose and staggered behind Dunne. They took a few tentative steps toward the church. The gunners did not open fire, and it occurred to Dunne that maybe he and Peters and Highway would not die in the ensuing moments.

"We surrender," Dunne called. "We give up.

You can goddamn have us."

The gunners continued peering at them.

"Got one injured," Dunne yelled while waving his gun barrel. "And one dead. We surrender. We give up."

Dunne took another step toward them, and another, and suddenly the gunners were yelling in German and Dunne thrust his hands higher in the air and yelled, "What? What is it?" Then he noticed that the Germans were pointing behind him and that they were tightening their grips on their weapons. Dunne turned and saw what had alarmed them. Peters was grinning—impishly, childishly—and had started to take off his rucksack.

"Peters," barked Dunne. "What the hell are you doing?"

The Fritz gunners were yelling now, while gesturing that Peters should lower the rucksack. Dunne moved well aside, his hands still thrust high into the air; he thought that maybe Peters couldn't see the effect his movements were having on their captors, though of course this didn't work. Despite Dunne moving out of his way, Peters was still smiling and saying, "I'm going home, I'm going home," while proceeding to loosen the straps of his pack and looking up periodically to grin at Dunne and the German gunners and the weak sliver of sunlight knifing the dishwater skies.

"Peters," Dunne snapped. "Leave it alone. Get your hands up."

"I'm going home."

"No you're not. Put it *down*."

The gunners were yelling louder now, something staccato and forceful, and while Peters continued to fumble with his pack, his smile a beam of crazed thought, Dunne stretched his hands farther into the air and pleaded, "No, stop, please, Kamerad, Kamerad ..."

The gunners opened fire on the boy. Dunne fell behind a low wall just a few yards from the gaping church front and blankly watched Peters's body jerk and dance in a jet-black bullet spray. When Peters finally fell onto dust, Dunne pulled the pin from another Mills bomb and, without thinking about such things as survival or God or the possibility of more life, held it for longer than he should have and then lobbed the grenade toward the church altar. He dropped and held his ears and, for the briefest of moments, listened to the sorrowful whine of what he imagined would be his final thoughts; they were neither comforting nor profound nor poignant, and had much to do with stupid decisions and missed opportunities. The explosion ricocheted off whatever walls were still standing in the village, the sound growing dimmer and dimmer until it was replaced by a tremulous quiet.

Dunne waited for more fire. It didn't come. He heard a rustling of air and that was all. He knew this to be a trick, so he waited patiently, and when his death still didn't come he lifted his head above the thin wall and saw only smoke and raised cement dust and fallen Fritz bodies. He waited and then he rose and walked toward the small church. It was ten steps to the altar, where the enemy had erected the gun behind a mound of sandbags. The weapon now pointed at the floor of the church, though as Dunne cautiously moved up the aisle he saw a hand rise up to the stock and attempt to swivel it toward Dunne. It dropped uselessly away.

Dunne fixed a bayonet to the end of his rifle. He reached the altar. He now saw that three of the Huns were dead. The one survivor was lying among them, his breath coming in shallow, rasping pants. Dunne moved to him and stood over him. The Hun's tunic was soaked through with blood and viscera, though Dunne couldn't tell how much of it was his own and how much of it had splashed from the soldiers who had fallen next to him. The boy's eyes were a watery depthless blue; Dunne realized the soldier couldn't be more than sixteen or seventeen.

The boy reached up with a shaking, slight hand.

"Kamerad," he whispered.

He smiled. Dunne continued looking down at him. There was death everywhere, it was a presence flavouring the air, and Dunne felt it useless to resist its demands.

"Kamerad," the boy tried again.

And it was coming, he couldn't control it, that furious contempt for life and self that fuels all wars and allows them to flourish. Dunne's hands trembled and his heart raced and he had never felt more alive or conquering when, in a single vicious movement, he lifted his bayonet and plunged it into the smiling boy's face.

One second later, there was another explosion, and the whole of Dunne's world turned deafening and black.

CALGARY

ONE

S HE WAS THE ONLY NURSE scheduled to work that night and this suited her fine. In a small room next to the ward for shell-shocked soldiers, she put on a white overdress and bonnet and momentarily checked herself in a mirror run through with rivulets of silver. She was about to step into the ward when one of the nursing sisters entered the change room, where she would prepare to go home.

"Sarah."

"Sister."

"There's a new patient."

"Yes?"

"Bed four. They found him walking along a road near the front, wounded and AWOL and muttering to himself. He had a piece of shrapnel in his hip."

"Why is he here?"

"He was treated in a hospital in England. Then they shipped him home to us. He needs rest. And observation."

"I see," said Sarah.

"He's quiet, now. He won't give you any problems."

"His name, sister?"

"Michael Dunne. He was at Vimy too."

The ward was quieter at night, though there were those who were bothered by the low light, causing them to weep and suffer night sweats. These were the men who took up the majority of her time, for they called to her in soft, pleading voices and though she was not permitted to touch them she could soothe them by reminding them that they were safe, that they were home, and that the war was far, far away. Sometimes this helped. She gave out cups of strong black tea to those who found it helpful—sometimes it felt as though she spent half her night steeping bitter leaves and the other half emptying the bedpans filled as a result. For those who were truly bothered, there were large black pills that, within twenty minutes, turned the most agitated of men into silent, deeply breathing statues, their eyes as blank as amber. And for those who were suffering from physical pain, there were tablets of morphine—it seemed that every other soldier returning from the front was addicted or, at the very least, on his way to becoming so. Though she hadn't understood the craving for these small, chalky pills when she first started nursing, she understood now. They took all of your pain, be it emotional or physical or spiritual, and transported it to a far-off place where it could do nothing more than shimmer and amuse.

She had discovered this on a night when it was quiet on the ward, and the moans of her patients had turned to dead-of-night mumblings, and her sadness had registered as an ache in her bones. Around two or three o'clock in the morning, she'd found herself staring out one of the hospital windows, watching the sad cast of moonlight over the street outside. Something about the soft grey quality of the light made her feel chilled and frightened and missing those who had left her, and she'd felt the temptation to try one of the magic tablets the men never stopped asking her for, or talking about, or praying for in moments of solemn quiet. Minutes later, she succumbed.

It hardly seemed to matter; there were so many tablets on the ward that nobody counted them or monitored them in any way. In fact, when they so much as came close to running out, cartons of the drug would show up, as if materialized from the ether. It was a source of agitation for the nursing sisters that this medicine was more available than tourniquets, than new bedding, than fruit and fresh meat and the balls of cotton needed to separate ruptured skin from a dressing.

Her fingers had shaken as she put the pill to her mouth. In her nervousness, she'd breathed at the wrong moment, and for a moment the tablet had stuck in her throat before loosening itself and leaving a grainy burn she felt when she swallowed. She waited for a few minutes and then went back to her job, moving up and down the aisles, tending to those men having difficulty with terror and enuresis, almost forgetting she had taken the tablet until the moment came when she floated above the floorboards, and her body shrouded itself in a warmth of its own making, and the soldiers in the room turned to monkey-faced angels, and a spectral light shone from each of their beings.

SISTER BEATRICE HAD BEEN RIGHT about the new soldier. Throughout the night he lay unmoving and quiet, though it was true he had sad, stricken eyes that, like the eyes of so many soldiers returning from the front, always seemed open, even when he slept—it was easy to get the impression he was locked in a state of semi-consciousness. He had a scar that curved moonlike around the base of his nose and another near the underside of his chin. On the occasion that his hands lay on top of the blanket, Sarah noticed that they were marked by nicks and small gouges, and that one of the knuckles on his right hand looked misshapen, as though something had once crushed it. Deep lines snaked from the corners of his eyes, and in them Sarah saw the impact of time and things witnessed.

He asked for nothing, and was able to use the latrine at the end of the ward by himself. His movements were slow and deliberate, and Sarah wondered if it hurt him to move. He was thirty-seven years of age—she knew this from reading his file, a dossier that also described him as a sergeant and a recipient of a Distinguished Conduct Medal and, paradoxically, a deserter. Occasionally, late at night, when her rounds took her past his cot, she imagined she was being followed by those dark, mournful eyes. But then, whenever she looked, he was always peering up at the ceiling or turned the other way.

Sarah attributed this sensation—this feeling she was being watched—to the tablets she now had to take to feel normal.

On his fourth night in the hospital, the sergeant yelled in his sleep and sat straight up in his cot. By the time she reached him, he had lain back down and was breathing hard. The hollow between the tendons in his neck was damp. He licked his lips and shuddered. She looked at his eyes and felt as though she knew him, from another place and another time.

"Nurse," he said.

"You're all right now, sergeant. You were dreaming."

"Couldn't have been. I don't sleep."

"You don't so much, do you?"

"I suppose I was then."

"What were you dreaming about?"

For the longest time he didn't answer. She was about to turn and leave him, thinking he didn't want to be disturbed, when he muttered, "In Europe. They have these birds called kestrels there."

"You were dreaming of birds?"

"Maybe. Sometimes you'd look up from the trenches and they'd be up above you, soaring."

"I see," she said. She was twenty-eight years old and understood that the things you are unable to do can also be the things that inspire the most vivid of nightmares. "Go back to sleep now."

The following evening, she passed by his cot and noticed he was awake. This time, he did not look away as she neared. Though the ward was far from silent—in their sleep, the other men moaned and yammered and voiced stuttering thoughts—she nonetheless whispered.

"Sergeant."

He swallowed and said nothing.

"Is there something you need?"

"No."

"Are you sure?"

"Yes."

"Might a cup of tea help?"

He paused, thinking.

"Maybe."

There was a serving station at one end of the ward, and as Sarah walked toward it she was conscious of the sound of her feet against the floorboards and the coursing of her tablet-made thoughts. There was a sink, a paraffin burner, a kettle and a tin of sugar biscuits. She lit the burner and a flow of blue light advanced over the room until the gloom of the ward was tinged a cool pale lavender. She caught the kettle just before it whistled. After steeping the sergeant's tea in a mug, she put a few cookies on a saucer and carried them back through the ward. It was three o'clock in the morning and the world outside was so quiet it felt as though she and the sergeant must be the only people awake in their small western city.

She reached his cot. Dunne sat up and she handed him the tea and he took a slow, cautious sip. He returned the mug to his lap and looked up at her. In the semi-darkness of the room, she thought that his skin looked vaguely jaundiced.

"Tell me something," he said.

"All right."

"Doesn't your husband mind you working at night?"

She was about to answer—was close to saying, *I am unmarried, Mr. Dunne*—when a dim recollection of hospital policy regarding fraternization poked through her warm, jellied thoughts.

"Good night," she said. "When you've finished your tea, just put your cup on the floor beside you."

She turned and walked back to the nurses' station. For the rest of the evening she felt conscious of his silent, brooding wakefulness emanating from cot number four at the opposite end of the ward. As always, the room smelled of pine and dried blood and stale bedsheets; for some reason, on this long, awkward night, this scent bothered her, even made her feel a little dizzy. After a bit, she relented and took a second tablet, and slipped into a waking and colour-soaked dream.

For the next two nights, she did not have any contact with Sergeant Dunne. This was partly by design and partly owing to the fact that a group of soldiers, traumatized by the fighting in Belgium, had joined the ward—that night, and the night after, she was busy applying compresses and emptying bedpans and changing wet sheets and handing out pills inspiring a comalike slumber. Toward the end of the first night, one of the soldiers, a cadaverous boy with bulging pink eyes, got out of bed and loitered near the doors to the ward. She led him back to bed, only to see him get up and hang near the doors again. The third time he arose, he pushed through the doors when she wasn't looking, and if he was ever seen or heard from again Sarah didn't know about it.

In the middle of the second night, two of the soldiers got into a fight. None of the other patients attempted to stop it—some looked on blankly, others clamped palms to their ears and hid beneath the covers, others rooted for one of the combatants, thankful to have something to fracture the monotony. (The sergeant, she noticed, rolled over and sighed and looked away from the

27

fisticuffs.) Thankfully, Sarah was not alone that night—she was with an older nursing sister named Agnes, who called for Sarah and said, "Go, child, your legs are younger than mine."

Sarah ran down the cool, deserted Calgary street, her way lit by the moon and the moon only. When she reached the small constabulary unit at the end of the block, she was out of breath and conscious of the way her hair had broken free from the constraints of her headdress. The police ran ahead of her and hauled the fighting soldiers away. It was close to seven in the morning before the rest of the patients finally calmed down and Sarah was allowed to trudge home, exhausted and sore, to the rickety house she shared with her younger brother, David.

The next night was quieter. Midway through her shift, she was walking down the ward's centre aisle when he called for her. His voice had a low, raspy, settled-in quality that sounded both familiar and harsh.

"Nurse."

She stopped and took a deep breath and approached.

"Yes, sergeant?"

"Tomorrow."

"Yes?"

"I'm going before the medical review board.

Seems I'm either crazy or a traitor or both. They'll figure out which one and then tell me. I'll be gone by tomorrow night."

"I see."

"Tell me your name."

"You know I can't do that, Sergeant Dunne."

She shook her head slowly, her eyes focused on his. She was turning to leave when he reached out and took her gently by the wrist and said, again, "Please tell me."

In the few seconds it took her to say, "No, please," she could do nothing but savour the cold, rough sensation of his skin against hers.

TWO

THE SERGEANT SLEPT POORLY in darkness, his thoughts growing murky and confused; he never quite benefited from actual rest. It was his ears. Every sound in the hospital became part of a grey, transplanted reality—every movement a snapped twig in a forest, every voice the plea of a wounded soldier, every rustle the creep of an unseen foe. This happened only in absolute silence. At night, in the hush of the ward, his ears would ring as though assaulted by a barrage of artillery, and he would sink deeper into the shelter of his bedsheets, only to imagine that his feet were mired in a mixture of

rain and bloody clay. His nose, too, would fill with
the scent of decomposition. With the arrival of daylight, the sounds of the hospital coming alive would
replace the sounds produced by his own mind, and
he would slip into an hour or two of morbid slumber, in which he came across the German boy in the
pulpit again and again and again.

On his final morning in the ward, he awoke
suddenly, an aged hand upon his shoulder. His
eyes opened. One of the nursing sisters was at
his bedside, along with two recruits wearing
dull-green battlewear.

"Sergeant?" whispered the nurse.

"I'm awake."

"These men are here for you."

"I gathered as much."

His escorts were young and they looked nervous and the sister made them wait for Dunne to
eat a breakfast of powdered eggs and coffee. He
made sure to take his time. When the sergeant
was finished, he climbed out of bed and hunted
for clothes in the duffel he kept beneath his bed.
The recruits kept their eyes lowered as Dunne
changed into his soldier's uniform.

"You boys locals?"

"Yeah," said the taller of the two.

"Then that's the only thing we got in common."

He walked ahead of them, his duffel over his shoulder. As he made for the door at the end of the ward, he kept his eyes forward and did not, in any way, acknowledge the other patients. Upon reaching the door he stopped and turned.

"Wait," he said to the privates.

"What is it?"

"Wait."

Dunne strode toward the nursing sister who'd awoken him; she was at her station, assembling a meal tray with hands that had grown gnarled and somewhat trembling with age.

"Nurse," he said.

"Yes, sergeant?"

"You know the nurse who works here at night? The younger one?"

The woman thought. "She is a volunteer?"

"Yes," Dunne answered. "Probably."

The woman thought again, her face suddenly lightening. "Yes, yes. I know the one you mean."

"What is her name?"

"I'm afraid I can't …"

"Please," he said. "Please."

There was a moment's hesitation, during which the sister seemed to peer through Dunne and understand each of his intentions and foibles.

"It's Sarah," she said in a lowered voice. "Sarah Mann."

"I'm thankful, sister."

With that he turned and headed toward his military accompaniment. He passed them and pushed through the doors. The day outside was a contradiction of cool, late-summer air and warm sunlight. The street was hard-packed and sturdy and not at all like the trenches of Belgium. As the sergeant walked, he kept his eyes down. The sight of so many people attending to life during wartime—greengrocers, schoolchildren, a traffic cop spewing orders, a Chinese launderer railing at an assistant, the elderly—filled Dunne with a contempt he was not at all proud of. He shuddered. There had been times when he'd looked out the window of the shell-shock ward at the rest of the city and, for a second or two, believed that what he saw was an illusion, no more real than the jerky, black-and-white cast of a movie projector.

"We're going to military headquarters," said one of the privates.

"I know that," said Dunne.

He did not look back or otherwise speak to the privates. At Centre Street, he turned and entered a large, chilly building made from brick turned black with wear. He waited in the lobby, surrounded by framed photographs of judges and premiers in robes. His escorts caught up to him

34

and the taller one, who sounded out of breath, said, "This way, sir."

He followed them to a courtroom about three-quarters of the way down the hall; he entered and sat on a dark-wood bench toward the back of the room. As per military protocol, the privates sat on either side of him. There were other soldiers like him—mostly AWOLs and discipline cases—sitting all around him, waiting to appear before two men at the front of the room. He did not pay attention, and within minutes he grew bored and frustrated and wished he was anywhere but here. This sensation—of wishing he was anywhere his own self *wasn't*—was one he'd started experiencing upon his return from the front. Whenever it struck, he found himself fantasizing about a return to the war, where, if nothing else, all things radiated a grim authenticity.

He thought he heard his name. One of the privates nudged him and whispered, "Sir, that's you."

Dunne rose and left his bag with his escorts. He approached the front of the tribunal and stood where all of the others had addressed the court. One of the officiating men was bearded and round-faced, and he smiled politely at Dunne. The other was slightly older and had a lean, sour-looking face.

"Sergeant Michael Dunne?" said the younger man.

"Sir."

"My name is Dr. Bernard, and this is my colleague Dr. Walker. We'll be presiding over your case today."

Dunne remained silent. He looked toward an expanse of panelled wall between the two physicians.

"Well," interjected Dr. Walker. "What do you have to say?"

"What is it I'm supposed to say?"

"There's no formula here," said Dr. Bernard. "We're just talking. You want to tell me about your nightmares? It says here you suffer from nightmares."

"No sir. In fact, I barely sleep, sir."

There was a long pause, during which the doctors looked at each other. It was Dr. Walker who finally spoke. "They say German soldiers nailed a Canadian NCO to a barn door during a retreat outside of Ypres. You were there, were you not?"

"I did take part in that retreat, sir, but I'm telling you if they had time to stop and nail a guy to a door they're better than I know them to be."

"Are you saying it didn't happen?"

"Rumours run fast at the front, sir. They've

clocked it: four hours from the Alps to the Channel."

There was another pause.

"Michael," Dr. Bernard finally said. "You are a decorated soldier."

"I received a DCM, sir, for killing a young German soldier following an ambush. It's not something I'm proud of."

"And you were injured in this exchange?"

"There was an explosion following that incident, sir. I don't remember anything that ensued."

Dr. Walker interjected. "Well it seems, sergeant, that you abandoned your command. It *seems* that you wandered away, wounded, heading for God knows where."

"That's probable, sir."

"Probable?"

"Like I say, my memory of the event is hazy at best."

"That may be, sergeant, but it's still insubordination. Some would say treason."

"I understand that, sir."

"Tell me, soldier. Do you remember being arrested? On the side of that road near Arras?"

"That I do, sir."

"But you don't remember what happened *between* the explosion and that moment?"

"That is correct, sir."

"Help us out here," said Dr. Bernard, the tops of his cheeks slightly flushed. "We are trying to determine your status of discharge. Your physical wounds have healed, that much is clear, yet if we give you a clean bill of health you'll be sent back to the field and face a desertion trial and most likely be executed."

"I figure I'll be going back one way or another."

"Are you saying you want to die, son?"

"I'm saying it's probably going to work out that way."

Dr. Bernard leaned forward slightly. "Michael. I'm trying to save your life."

Dunne didn't respond.

"All right," said Dr. Walker. "You may sit."

Dunne backed toward a bench at the front of the seating area. In the ensuing silence, his ears filled with gunfire and the howls of frightened men. To distract himself, he watched as the two physicians leaned toward each other and began conferring. It seemed to Dunne that Dr. Bernard did most of the talking—he was gesturing with his hands as though attempting to convince the other doctor of something unpalatable. In the end, the lean-faced doctor rolled his eyes and crossed his arms over his chest and sat back in his chair, as though refusing to participate. Dr. Bernard spoke for a few seconds more and then began to write something on a sheet of paper. This went on for minutes and minutes.

Finally, Dr. Bernard looked up and said, "Sergeant, you may approach."

Dunne rose and took a few steps toward the physicians' table. Dr. Bernard spoke.

"It is the decision of this tribunal that you are suffering from neurasthenia and are unfit to return to battle. We are recommending that you be assigned to the 10th Battalion Recruitment Office, where you will support our ongoing effort. Do I make myself clear?"

"Sir."

"Approach, soldier."

Dunne neared the doctors.

"Here," said Dr. Bernard. "Take this. It is your medical report. Keep it with you at all times. It justifies your non-combat position."

He handed over a piece of paper. Dunne took it and quartered it and put it in the outer breast pocket of his jacket.

"Dismissed," said Dr. Bernard.

THE SERGEANT SPENT THE AFTERNOON looking for a place to stay, eventually finding a hostel run by a Ukrainian woman. He selected a room at the rear of the second floor that contained a bed, a dresser and a desk with chair; when he crossed the wide-planked floor, columns of dust sifted into the air. The window looked out onto an alley and the black-brick wall of the house next door.

"I'll take it."

"There are others," said the landlady.

"This one's fine."

Dunne paid her two weeks' worth of rent in advance from his pension money. When the landlady left, he changed out of his uniform and lay on top of the bedspread and watched the low, rain-soaked clouds of Belgium drift across the ceiling above him. Outside, the sun slowly sank beneath the mountains, turning the city a pale dusky blue. After a time, Dunne rose and found a cafeteria on Centre Street, where he ate a meatloaf supper at a table by himself. By the time he was finished, it was dark outside, and the sergeant thought about looking up his old friend Royster, with whom he worked for a while in a sawmill near Canmore. He lit a cigarette and started walking and gave the plan some more consideration. A few minutes later, he came across an unmarked speak he knew from before. It was filled mostly with servicemen and a few working women with sad, searching faces. After having a few drinks at the bar, he asked the bartender if he could buy a bottle of rum to take with him.

"It'll cost you."

"I have money."

He took the bottle and went down to the Bow River. Though it took him a while, he eventually found the place where he used to fish and hunt frogs as a boy. Here he sat and uncapped the bottle and looked up at the night sky before taking his first long swallow. It was better rum than had reached the European front, and he smiled at the way it warmed his throat and stomach without causing either to burn unduly. He took another swallow, and another. He thought of friends in Europe, mostly those who'd been killed. He also thought of the nurse named Sarah Mann, the one with the dazed green eyes and a fatigued prettiness. She was hooked on morphine, that much was clear, and this made him want to know her all the more. He also wondered if he'd ever see her again. Though the war had done something injurious to his desire for women, he promised himself that he would.

The stars began to meld into a wash of silver, undulating light. Dunne lay on his back and heard the voices of people he'd known in his life begin to swirl in the air, until they, too, blended together and grew to sound like the chatter of ghosts.

He drank much of the bottle and then rose and staggered back to his rooming house, where his landlady confronted him with rules regarding curfew and alcohol; Dunne was conscious only of the streaks her waving finger made in the air and of a bleary, dark mole on one side of her face. In the end she said she'd give Dunne another chance *only* because she'd heard he was a decorated soldier and a hero for something he'd done in Europe.

"Thank you, ma'am," he said, though it was true he had only picked her gloomy and mould-ridden establishment so that he wouldn't be disappointed when she did ask him to leave. He passed her and went to his room and flopped into bed. He slept in work jeans and a flannel shirt. When he came to the next morning, it was late and his mouth was dry and the front of his head thudded with every movement. He showered in the communal bathroom, dressed in his uniform, and walked three blocks to the recruitment office.

For the longest time, he stood on the opposite side of the street, looking at a banner urging men to do their duty and enlist. He finally took a deep breath and smoothed his hair and crossed the street. Inside the office, he found a slim blond man at a table and a few dirty-faced enlistees in the waiting room, looking nervously at one another. It was a far cry, Dunne thought, from the beginning of the war, when young men, all of them strapping and clean-living and sturdy, had descended upon recruitment offices by the thousands. Dunne had even seen them fight one another to get a better place in line.

A portly officer with a handlebar moustache approached him, a hand outstretched. Dunne took it.

"Ah," the man said. "You must be Dunne, if I'm not mistaken. I'm Major Dobson-Hughes. Come, come. I'm glad to see you. We need some new blood around here. No slight intended to my predecessor, but the sails on this ship are slack. The home front is awash in saboteurs and provocateurs—odd those words sound French, what? Allies and all. Be that as it may, our immediate concern at this juncture is, of course, recruitment."

He gestured toward the waiting room.

"As you can see, we are no longer getting what you'd call the pick of the litter. Shame, really."

Dunne followed Dobson-Hughes as he strolled around the perimeter of the office. The major kept talking. "Minimum age, eighteen. Infantry, service and medical corps: minimum height, five foot, three inches; chest thirty-three and one-half inches. Gunners: minimum height, five foot, seven inches. Give or take, you understand. But most of all, I encourage you to use your discretion. Exceptions are allowable. Remember—recruitment *is* a priority. We do what we have to do. That's always been my motto, and it's one that served me well in Africa. This, by the way, is Carmichael."

They had stopped next to the thin blond man.

"Feet as flat as a floorboard, isn't that right, Carmichael? And myopic to boot."

"That's correct, sir."

"He'll never serve in this man's army. Unless, of course, things become *truly* dire. Carmichael, this is Sergeant Dunne. He is our new recruitment officer."

"Welcome."

Before Dunne could respond, Dobson-Hughes led him away and continued speaking.

"As I was saying, preference given to unmarried men. The blind and the deaf are to be avoided, and asthmatics are strictly ne touche pas, given the problems associated with gas. Otherwise, it's pretty much an open-door policy."

He stopped and gestured toward the Boer War ribbon on his tunic. He spoke in a lowered voice. "I've seen acts of depravity, Dunne. Kroonstad. You've heard of it, no doubt. Human depravity. Absolute butchery. Disgusting. But *gas*? Even the Boer would not sink so low."

"We use gas too, sir."

Dobson-Hughes paused and let his eyes travel up and down Dunne's torso.

"I beg your pardon."

"We use it too."

The officer's face soured. He leaned toward Dunne. "I might as well make one thing clear, sergeant. I've read your dossier. I know about your, ahem, *medical* status. Assigning you here was not my idea."

"Yes sir."

"Then we understand each other ... right, take a seat next to Carmichael ... Local time? 8:57 a.m. Battlefield time? 4:57 p.m. No rest for the wicked. Let's get this show on the road, what? No time like the present, I should say ..."

Dunne sat. The first to approach his station was a young, gangly man with a bobbing Adam's apple and a halo of earth-brown freckles scattered across the tops of his cheekbones. He was about six feet, three inches tall, and if he weighed more than one hundred and twenty pounds it wasn't by much; Dunne wanted to reach across the table and shake him by the shoulders and tell him to *think* about what he was about to do. Instead, he cleared his throat and, reading from a questionnaire, asked, "Name?"

"George Andrew Crawley, sir."

"Age?"

"Twenty-one years, sir."

"Have you ever been convicted of a criminal offence?"

"No sir."

"Have you ever been a member of a criminal organization, or any organization with designs to unseat the government of either Canada or any other Commonwealth nation?"

"No sir."

"Are you a homosexual?"

"No sir."

"Do you have any medical conditions that would prevent your duties as a soldier?"

"I don't believe so, sir."

"Report to the medical office. Second door on the right. Remove your clothes to your underwear and wait."

The man moved on, and Dunne saw the next applicant. His third came around ten-thirty in the morning. The fourth didn't come in till after lunch.

HIS LIFE BECAME MADDENINGLY DULL, and he yearned for a way out. He drank in the evenings and came to work in an aching, somnolent haze. During the day, he would process the volunteers, the only break from the monotony coming at lunch, when he would eat a sandwich in the park and watch the civilians go about their lives as best as they were able, given that so many had husbands and brothers and fathers fighting overseas. This tired him, and he reported back to work with a diffused anger. Then it would all start again, each enlistee, it seemed, bearing a different variation of the same story. While it was true that some were healthy, sandy-haired boys with dreams of glory, this description more characterized the enlistees of 1914, 1915 and even 1916. This was 1917, and the men Dunne enlisted were different. They were hard-living mountain men, attracted by the proposition of three square meals a day. They were stick-thin prairie dwellers, tired of getting their clothes from church basements. They were tattooed criminals, on the run from dangerous people. They were shaky, unshaven men who saw war as an end to long, long stretches of bad luck. They were randy teenagers, scrawny and underage, with ill-found plans to impress a girlfriend (and maybe, *maybe*, finagle a goodbye they could tell the other soldiers about). They were gamblers running from debt; they were grubby small-towners who'd made enemies with the wrong people; they were bearded old-timers with Eastern European accents; they were young men of God who viewed the Hun as a threat to things saintly. They were misfits, cow wranglers, grifters, card sharps, horse thieves, five-finger artists and sellers of questionable insurance

47

policies. Dunne wished he could help each one of them.

He asked them a single question after writing down all of their answers.

"You like sleeping in mud and getting shot at?"

"I beg your pardon?"

"Simple question. You like sleeping in mud and getting shot at or don't you?"

Every last one of them gave the same answer, which was the answer they thought Dunne wanted to hear: *Yes sir, if it means killing Germans* or *Yes sir, if it means we can live in a free country* or, simply, *Yes sir, I do.* After a while, Dunne didn't hear it. He started viewing them all as a single entity, as a sad and unending procession. He grew to hate the work he was doing, and the reason he was doing it.

"One last question."

"Yes sir."

Dunne would look up and peer at the enlistee through morose, heavy-lidded eyes. "You positive you *want* to do this?"

Often it was a question that seemed to catch the enlistee off guard, as though his own wishes mattered little in the progression of his own life. This didn't surprise Dunne, for he knew all about living by this way of thinking. When the enlistee finally answered, it was generally after a considerable pause, and with a slight tremulousness in his voice.

"Yes sir," he would say. "I'm pretty sure I do."

THREE

THE YOUNG MAN lay atop the love of his life, kissing her mouth and running his hands through her hair and fighting with the buttons that ran, like a march of small coins, down the front of her bodice. When he finally ran out of air, he lifted his mouth from hers and said, "I think maybe I should take this opportunity to underscore the elusive relationship between desire and social order."

Cassie laughed and straightened her clothes while, at the same time, hugging him closer to her.

"You're crazy, David Mann."

They kissed again, their mouths a fevered compression, a warmth transmitting through clothing and skin and blood. They stopped only when they heard a voice come from the outer office.

"David?" the voice called. "*David?*"

"Shit," the boy whispered while leaping off Cassie. "It's Mackinnon."

"Oh no," Cassie said, and they both cowered behind David's desk in the back room of *The Calgary Independent*. From here, they listened as Mackinnon continued to call his employee's name while pacing the front-office floors. When there was no response, he spat, "Oh bugger," and then David and Cassie heard the front door open and shut, meaning that Mackinnon had probably stepped outside to list the day's top stories on the sandwich board.

David laughed and said, "Come on."

He leapt up and grabbed Cassie by the hand and they both ran for the rear door, knocking over a garbage can in the process. By the time they reached the grassy pitch extending behind the building, they were both bent over and laughing so hard they could barely catch their breath. After a moment, they stood and looked, eyes streaming, at each other. Cassie was grinning, and he could spot the incisor on the right side of her mouth. For some reason this made him love her all the more.

At the end of the property there was a wild-flower meadow and, beyond that, a coldwater stream that started somewhere in the foothills. Cassie turned and lifted her billowing skirt and ran across the field. David sped after her. Soon they found a place at the stream where others had placed stepping stones; they dampened their feet as they crossed it and then entered a pasture growing with twitch grass and daisies and wheat. They slowed to a walk. The sky was an endless blue. David noticed that Cassie was running the palms of her hands over the tops of the wheat stalks and that the sensation was making her thoughtful.

"I think maybe Daddy knows about us," she said.

"No kidding."

"What do we do?"

"I better talk to him."

"Don't be stupid, David. You can't just *talk* to Daddy. Besides ..."

"Besides what?"

"He doesn't like you."

"I haven't even met him yet."

"He doesn't like the idea of you."

"That's why I have to talk to him. He'll come around."

They walked in silence. David could hear birds and insects and his own soaring thoughts.

"You'd do that?" she finally said.

"I would."

"He can be … formidable."

"I'm aware of that, yes."

"So you *will* talk to him?"

"Yes."

"You'd do that for me?"

Before he could answer—before he had time to say, Don't you know, Cassie? I'd scale mountains for you, I'd hunt lions for you, I'd walk over burning coals for you and you only—she stopped and turned and unfastened the top three buttons on her blouse. David grinned and touched her gently, his fingertips tracing the impression made by the clavicle against her soft, china-white skin. Cassie permitted this for a second, only to squeal and lift her skirt and run from him laughing. David pursued her down a small hill that led toward the edge of the woods, and when he finally caught her they both fell in a grasping heap. As he kissed her, he noticed they'd attracted the attention of a young deer, who regarded them through blinking, huge eyes before darting toward a grove of spruce and old cedar.

He could smell grass and Cassie's shampoo, and as his nose pressed into the recess between her chin and neck he could also detect the faintest aroma of sweat and this excited him further. His pelvis ground against hers, his hands roamed her clothed body. When he shifted his weight to one side, so as to lift the frilled edge of her skirt, her eyes popped wide open and she grabbed his wrist and sharply said, "No!" Still, he persisted, telling Cassie he loved her and he cherished her just as he cherished light and fresh air, yet when he again tried to lift the hem of her skirt she pushed his hand away and commanded him to stop, only this time she did so with the slightest tinge of alarm in her voice. He immediately rolled off her, his burning defused by a measure of shame.

"I'm sorry," she said while fastening her buttons.

"It's all right."

"I'm not ready."

"I know."

Her hand touched his; he responded by holding it gently. For the longest time, they lay looking up at the sky, saying nothing. Above, through a sway of branches, he saw blue sky and hawks and a lazy passing of clouds.

"David," she finally said.

"Yes?"

"Would you really talk to my father?"

THAT NIGHT, DAVID MANN WAITED FOR SARAH to leave for her nursing job at the military hospital. When he finally heard the tap of hobnail boots against the stairs, he dressed in his only suit. Though it gripped him around the chest and showed a surfeit of wrist when he lifted his arms, it had been one of the last things his father had bought him and in this there was a measure of comfort. He looked at himself in a mirror clouded with age. His skin was lit amber by the throw of lamplight in the room. Though he was no judge of what made one man handsome and another homely, he was satisfied with the reflection that greeted him.

He left their battered little home whistling.

It was a long walk into the centre of town, to the neighbourhood along the Bow River where the town's wealthy kept homes as large as city blocks. To reach there, he walked through parts of Calgary where Chinese families lived three to a room. Here, smudge-faced characters watched from alcoves as you passed by, refuse collected against the facades of soot-darkened buildings, and women with their hair pinned high called out from the open windows of saloons. To calm his nerves, he stepped into one of these establishments and walked through air curdled with smoke. At the bar he ordered a rye whisky, and when the barkeep asked if he was old enough to drink, David replied, "Yep, but not old enough to know better." This made the publican laugh and he poured David a small beer to go with it.

"Might as well have something to chase it with," the man said. "Go to it, kid."

"I'm obliged," said David, and he used the beer to cool the burning of the whisky. As he drank, he kept noticing women in bustiers looking at him and smiling, and he was glad he was savvy enough to know what they were after. One even came up to him and said, "What's a nice boy like you doing in a dump like this?" In response, he raised a hand and said, with a grin, "Nothing you need to know about."

When he left a minute later, his courage was on equal footing with his optimism. He whistled as he entered the city's downtown core, though he made sure to detour around the newspaper offices just in case Mackinnon spotted him and wanted to know why he hadn't made it to work that day. He kept walking. Around him were three- and four-storey brick buildings grown silent with the onset of dark. The tall buildings gave way to mature trees and groomed lawns and stretches of wrought-iron fencing. He was alone now and conscious of the sound of his boot heels echoing off the packed earth of the roadway. Far off a dog howled, and for some reason the loneliness in the animal's yowling shook David's nerve a little, and he wished he'd stayed for another round with the amused bartender. By the time he reached Cassie's house, a three-storey rise of turrets and white porches and gingerbread accents, he noticed that his palms had grown slightly damp; only his feelings for Cassie, and his trust in his own charm, kept him going. He pushed through a high, wrought-iron gate that made him think, for just a second, about the fallen women back at the saloon and the sort of lives they must lead in cold, well-worn rooms. As per Cassie's instructions, he crept around the back of the house and tapped at the door to the kitchen.

He waited. He tapped again, this time a little more forcefully. The oval face of their Chinese cook filled the window in the upper half of the door.

"What you want?" she called through the glass.

Before David could answer, Cassie was there, saying, "It's all right, Mrs. Chang. It's for me."

She opened the door. David stepped inside and she straightened his black hair and kissed him chastely on the cheek. He smiled devilishly.

"So," he said. "Why the back-door treatment?"

"I wanted to make sure you looked okay."

"Do I?"

She smiled. "You look handsome."

"The suit's too small."

"It shows off your muscles."

"I don't have any."

"Yes you do. Now, remember, always look Daddy in the eye. And if he offers his hand, give him a firm handshake. He'll respect you for it. And don't voice any anti-war sentiment."

"I have none to voice." Again, he smirked. "Anything else?"

"Call him Dr. Walker. Or sir."

"Got it."

David's bow tie was slightly askew; when Cassie reached up to adjust it, she bore the faint trace of a grin. She took a deep breath, threw back her shoulders and asked if he was ready. He told her he was.

They walked hand in hand along a wood-panelled hallway, occasionally passing rooms into which David's entire house could have fit. They took a left and then a right and then another left, and it occurred to David that, should Cassie faint or collapse for some reason, he'd be unable to return to the kitchen by himself.

She stopped before a dark wooden door near the end of a hallway toward the side of the house. She knocked.

"Yes?" came the voice from inside.

"Daddy?"

"Yes?"

"David's here."

There was a pause.

"Show him in."

She pushed open the door and David followed her into a large, wood-faced library. Dr. Walker sat behind an oak desk, which was scattered with papers. He put down his pen and looked up and attempted the thinnest vestige of a smile. He stood.

"So, Cassie. At last we meet your friend David …"

David came forward. "It's good to meet you, sir."

David took the older man's hand and squeezed it until the small muscles near the wrist issued complaint.

"And it's good to meet *you*, young man. Please, please. Have a seat."

There were a pair of wooden armchairs facing the doctor's desk; David and Cassie each took one while Cassie's father sat again behind the imposing barrier that was his desk.

"So, he said. "Cassie tells me you're a newspaperman."

"In a manner of speaking, sir."

David grinned, though when Dr. Walker didn't follow suit he sobered.

"So you're a scribe, then?"

"Well," responded David. "Not a scribe, exactly."

"He's a typesetter, Daddy."

The doctor raised an eyebrow at David. "A typesetter?"

"Yes, sir."

"You set ... *type*?"

"I do."

"And do you foresee yourself doing this in the future?"

"No, sir. It's just something ..."

"Yes?"

"It's more of something I'm doing for now."

Cassie's father touched his fingertips together and, for a moment, gazed over the tops of David and Cassie's heads.

"So tell me. What *are* your plans?"

"My plans?"

"Yes, young man. Your plans."

David looked at the doctor, a man with as solid a reputation as it is possible to have, and realized he had nothing to tell him. It also occurred to him that all things could not be accomplished by quick thinking and an easy smile, and that, furthermore, there was something to be said for preparedness and rigour. Sitting there, wordless, David suddenly realized that he'd taken a large step toward this ephemeral conceit known as maturity, his only regret being that it was happening now, in the presence of Cassie's frowning and judgmental father (who, David was also in the process of realizing, had a face like a distempered ferret). With no decent cards to lay on the table, he decided to enact a strategy he relied on rarely and tell the man something close to the truth.

"Well, I've always had an interest in astronomy."

"*Astronomy?*"

"Yes sir. I've always been interested in, well, constellations."

"And where would you, er, *pursue* this course of study? On some mountaintop somewhere?"

"That's generally where the best observatories are."

"It's a noble pursuit," Cassie interjected.

"So you and Cassie … should your, mmm, dalliance continue … would go to live atop some mountain, where you would spend your days looking at stars?"

"I suppose, sir."

"I'd imagine you'd have to do this under the auspices of some academic institution, yes? A university graduate course, perhaps?"

"I would, sir."

"And before you'd do this, you'd have to acquire an undergraduate degree, am I correct?"

David, who understood that the trap into which he had fallen was only going to grow more diabolical and ensnaring, could only swallow and say, "You are."

"The course of study would be astrophysics, am I correct?"

"Yes, sir."

"So tell me, David. To what universities have you applied?"

David slumped in his seat; the truth was that he'd decided to take a year off following his graduation from high school, a decision that had felt reasonable at the time but now seemed to indicate indolence and lack of direction. He risked a glance at Cassie and found that even she seemed annoyed by his fecklessness. He felt speechless and defeated and stupid, and he was about to excuse himself when he glanced up at his adversary and saw a certain lightening of gravity displayed like a beacon on the doctor's pinched, narrow face. Though he mistrusted the sudden presence of this lifeline, he nevertheless accepted it with an unspoken gratitude.

Cassie's father, meanwhile, opened his hands, as if to show that he had nothing to hide.

"My boy," he said. "Tell me. How old are you?"

"Seventeen, sir."

"And might I ask why you are not dressed in a soldier's garb? There *is* a war on, you know."

David glanced downward. "I turn eighteen in three months. It was something I was considering ..."

"Listen to me," the good doctor continued. "I was once like you. Floundering, at loose ends, not a clue what I wanted to do in this life."

"Daddy!" yelped Cassie.

"Please, Cassie. Your friend and I are laying our cards on the table. Isn't that right, David?"

"Yes, sir."

Dr. Walker leaned forward on the desk.

"I did a year of military duty. It did me a world of good. Taught me discipline, forbearance, a love of my country. It gave me my bearings."

"Daddy," Cassie interjected. "There's a war on!"

"All the better. His country needs him. It has always been my regret that I served during peacetime. As for his age ... well. I wouldn't dwell on it too much. I have it on good authority that the recruitment officers have been instructed to be somewhat lenient, in view of current enlistment figures."

He turned back to David.

"Try a year, young man. Then you and I can talk about any intentions you might have toward my daughter. And by the way, if I'm not mistaken, there's a whiff of alcohol on your breath, and the army will help you with any problem you might have in that direction as well."

THE FOLLOWING MORNING, David Mann showered and shaved the slight layering of down that had collected on his lip and chin over the last week or so. He then had coffee and nothing else, and walked to the 10th Battalion Recruitment Office downtown. Here, he waited in a chilly room with two others, his excitement growing with each passing minute—It was the right thing to do. It was the least he could do for his country—until finally his number was called and he approached an older, dark-haired sergeant with a distant, hollow cast to his eyes.

"Name?"

"David Mann."

"Age?"

"Eighteen," David lied.

The officer looked up at David.

"*Mann?*"

"Yes. That's right."

"Do you by any chance have a sister? Who works as a nurse in the military hospital?"

"I do."

The man seemed to be thinking.

"What is your address?"

"58 Barrow Street."

"And where is that, son?"

"On the edge of town."

The sergeant was studying David. His eyes narrowed and in so doing he looked angered. "You're eighteen?"

"I am."

"You look awful seventeen to me, kid."

"I'm eighteen!"

"You got something that says so?"

"I didn't know I had …"

"Listen to me, kid. I'm looking at you and I'm thinking you're a long way from eighteen and so long as I'm sitting at this desk you will not be going to this war."

"But …"

"But nothing, young man. Get out of this office."

"Sergeant, I …"

"*Next*, goddamn it."

David Mann turned. His face felt warm, as though he'd been struck. He walked along the bustling street. He'd never felt more useless. He bought an apple and couldn't eat more than a few bites so he threw it high in the air, over the top of a row of building fronts. By the time he reached the end of the block, he was beset with the belief that every conversation occurring around him, and every snippet of laughter reaching his reddened ears, was about him and this inexplicable failure.

FOUR

DUNNE LEFT WORK just after dusk's fall.
Instead of taking a trolley, he decided he
needed fresh air and the movement of his legs.
The sky was topped with a mat of dense cloud. He
walked through streets turned grey in low light;
as he neared his rooming house, the streets turned
quiet, infested with stray dogs and transients. In
his ears he heard the whisperings of ghosts and
those who had fallen dead in trenches and on
muddy Belgian roadways. Every block, he turned
and checked that he wasn't being pursued, only

to remember where he was and feel stupid. By the time he reached his room, his head was ringing with thought, and he was suffering, yet again, from the impression that his surroundings—the chipped wooden floorboards, the faded yellow wallpaper, the scent of cabbage and mildew—were the product of a persistent, unpleasant dream.

He passed his landlady in the hallway. She handed him a fresh set of towels and he thanked her. With his hands full, he fumbled to retrieve the latchkey from his pocket. He jiggled it and the lock finally gave and he stepped into a room steeped in darkness. When he felt a thick, coated arm wrap around his throat and squeeze, there was a moment, however fleeting, when he believed that the arm and the sensation of pain were somehow a product of his own damned imagination. He blinked twice, and then it came to him—the realization that air wasn't reaching his lungs—and when the sides of his head began to pound he understood that this moment was actually happening, he really *was* being attacked, and so he lifted a boot and planted it hard in his attacker's shin. This caused his killer's grip to loosen so Dunne pushed backward with his legs, slamming the unseen man hard into the wall. He heard air leave the man's lungs, and when this translated into a further loosening of the grip around his throat, the sergeant spun and jammed his hand in a pocket to reach the switchblade he carried at all times. He sprung it and held it to the man's throat—in the darkness he could see the man was large and bearded and missing one arm—and would have slit the man's throat had he not heard laughter and the sound of his landlady banging on the door.

"What is going on in there?" she yelled in her thick Ukrainian accent.

"Nothing," Dunne called as the man kept chortling. "Nothing."

"Then what's all that crashing around in there?"

"It's nothing," Dunne said as he let the man go. "I'm sorry."

"I don't allow this sort of thing."

"I know," called Dunne. "I'm sorry."

He listened to the sound of the landlady's heavy footfalls receding along the hallway, and then Dunne was chuckling as well. He stepped over his dropped hand towels and lit the lantern on his bedside table.

"Jesus, Royster," he said. "I coulda killed you."

"And I coulda killed you."

"I'm glad you showed me that courtesy. What happened to your arm?"

"Lost it in the sawmill. Sad, ain't it?"

"Makes me glad I moved on."

"Makes me wish you hadn't."

"How'd you get in here?"

"Picked the lock with a wire. Comes in handy."

"Probably works better than my key."

The two men laughed and looked at each other. It was the first time Dunne had laid eyes on a face that preceded his days in Europe since he'd been home, and for this small pleasure he was grateful.

Royster spoke. "Could we get drunk now, *please*?"

"Ain't you heard? It's a dry province."

"About as dry as you are. Let's go."

The two men paused at the door of Dunne's room and listened for the landlady. When they heard nothing they crept down the hallway, though by the time they reached the stairs they had forgotten about her and their feet fell hard against the frayed runner, sending reverberations through the house so that the last thing they heard before leaving the house was, "Please, Sergeant Dunne, I've told you …"

Once in the street they headed toward Chinatown.

"Ah, Mikey," said Royster. "I figured you for dead over there. I'm glad to see you ain't. You'll like civilian life. There's no shortage of women, all free and clear and every one of them more than interested in lifting their skirts. You know why?"

"You give 'em money."

"That's the beauty of it. *I don't have to.* 'Stead I let them know they're in the presence of a war hero."

"When did you become a war hero?"

"When I lost my goddamn arm. By the way, I got a postcard from Highway."

"From *Highway*? Jesus ..."

"Seems he's back on his feet and tearing a swath through London. Wanted to know what happened to you."

"What did you tell 'im?"

"Haven't answered yet. I'll get to it now that I have an answer."

"I miss that crazy Indian."

"I miss him too."

They entered a speak called The Red Letter and went to the bar. There they were met by a barkeep whom Royster knew as Johnny. The room was filled with smoke and loud chatter and the smell of unwashed denim. Royster and Dunne both ordered whiskies and when they'd drained them they ordered two more.

"Jesus," Royster said. "It's good to see you in one piece."

"More or less," said Dunne.

Royster lifted the shot glass before him and eyed his old friend from the sawmill and said, "Here's to you."

"Thanks."

"Listen," said Royster. "What happened over there, anyway?"

"A lot happened over there."

"A lot or something specific?"

"Both."

"You don't talk about it."

"It's not what you do."

"I wouldn't either."

They drank and slammed their small glasses against the bar top and were about to call out to Johnny the barkeep when they heard a slurred voice behind them. Dunne turned and saw the kid he'd rejected that morning, the brother of that lost nurse named Sarah. He was about to say hello when he noticed that the kid was reeling and blind drunk and that his face was tightened with a mixture of rage and shame.

"Go home, kid."

"Look at you two. So jesusly rhetorical."

"Christ, Mikey. Who's this kid?"

"He's nobody. Go home."

"I gotta do something," mumbled David Mann.

"Look, I know."

"I gotta do something!"

"Jesus, kid, I know. Now fuck off."

"Mikey, what is this?"

"What is *this*?" raged David. "This ... war hero ..."

"I ain't no hero," Dunne mumbled.

"This hero said I was too young for the war."

At this Royster grinned and showed yellowing teeth and said, "Mikey, this true? I thought they took anybody who could walk these days."

"Long story," said Dunne.

The kid was reeling and gesturing and Dunne knew that trouble was not long off.

"Fuck off home, kid."

"I'm eighteen and you know it."

To make his point, David grabbed the front of Dunne's shirt. Dunne, in turn, grabbed a handful of David Mann's hair and pushed the side of his face into the beer-soaked bar, and when he had him there he lowered his mouth to within an inch of the boy's ear and yelled, "Goddamn it, kid. I was doing you a favour."

He let him go. David Mann stood, his face damp with spilled foam. His eyes were cold and dark and his nose apple-red. "Fuck you," he said once again, and when he staggered toward the door Dunne saw again the shape the boy was in.

"Damn," he murmured.

After giving it a half-minute's thought, he turned to Royster and said, "We better go."

"What do you care?"

"We better go."

Royster dropped some money on the bar and they wove through the crowd. When they found the boy outside he was bent over and puking into a gutter running with cigarette butts and the moisture of a recent downpour. Dunne walked up to the boy and put his hand on his arched, quaking back and said, "Let's get you home."

David stood and breathed deeply and said, "You should have enlisted me."

"I won't ever."

"Still, you should've."

"I won't."

An ice truck was approaching and Dunne stopped it by not moving from the street. When the driver began waving his arms and yelling in Chinese, Dunne moved toward him and said he'd give him five dollars to take himself and the drunk boy somewhere close. The Chinaman nodded. Dunne said goodbye to Royster, and ten minutes later he was helping the boy along the walk leading to the front door of the boy's house. Dunne stopped halfway and let the boy stumble the rest of the way himself.

As the kid fumbled with the lock, Dunne looked

at the house—peeling paint, slanted porch, windows curtained with old sheets—and he felt a kinship with the nurse who lived there that bordered on insistent. When David Mann made it into the house, Dunne turned and was preparing to walk home when he heard his name called. He turned back.

"Sergeant Dunne," Sarah called again.

She was wearing an old dress and her hair was ratty; there was a worn, settled-in beauty to her that made the sergeant feel at rest with himself. She walked up to him, her arms folded across the front of her body.

"I'm not sure whether I should be thanking you," she said.

"I figured you'd be at work."

"I'm not. What happened?"

"I ran into him."

"Where?"

"A place."

"The Red Letter, I'm thinking."

Dunne grinned slightly and in so doing gave Sarah her answer.

"What happened?"

"He had a small accident, is all."

She glanced back at the house and then grinned herself. "Looks like that accident was fist-shaped. I'm only hoping it wasn't yours."

"It's a bit of a story."

She paused and grinned again. "Well. I suppose in that case I should thank you for bringing him home."

"You don't have to."

"I'll thank you anyway."

"I don't suppose you and I could take a walk some afternoon."

"I don't walk with soldiers, sergeant."

"I could lose the uniform."

"I don't walk with naked soldiers, sergeant."

Dunne paused; he felt a tightening in his throat that was unbearable. "I am trying to make you like me."

"And I'm not making it easy."

"What if I asked your father for permission?"

"That would be difficult."

"He doesn't like suitors?"

"No. My father's dead. He was killed at Vimy."

Dunne looked at the ground. "Jesus. I'm sorry. I didn't know."

"Goodnight, Sergeant Dunne."

DUNNE WENT HOME FEELING WORSE than he had at the beginning of the evening. He lay awake, staring at his bedroom ceiling, his ears alive with the chatter of lost souls and his heart's doomed wishes. When he finally fell asleep in the early hours of the new day, he dreamt of the boy in the church near the Arras road, and it was in his sleep that he first realized that the boy looked a little like David Mann. He came awake bolt upright in a sticky, nauseating sweat, and he calmed himself by thinking of Sarah. It was still early on a Saturday morning, and the street outside his window had yet to come alive with newspaperboys and fishmongers and icemen and young nannies rushing off to the mansions near the Bow River. He dressed and went outside and turned toward the edge of town. The shops weren't open, so when he passed a general goods store he went around back and jimmied a door and helped himself to apples and a length of sturdy rope. He placed a few coins next to the large metal cash register and left.

He continued walking until the thoroughfare leading through the city forked and led to a series of soggy wagon ruts servicing the ranches and animal farms operating in the foothills of the mountains. Just after seven in the morning, he came to one fronted with a paddock of horses. The farmhouse itself was set well off toward the back of the property and, though it was light out, he was pretty sure the house itself was still dark. About half of the horses, upon seeing a stranger at this early hour, milled over to investigate.

Dunne looked in all directions and proceeded to the line of animals. Near an old metal gate, he offered a pair of sugar cubes he'd had in his pocket to a young, dust-coloured horse; when the horse tried to take the sugar cubes in Dunne's glove, a stallion came over and pushed the smaller horse aside, which was fine as it nudged it in the direction of the gate. Dunne walked in this direction as well, his hand outstretched and leading the stallion, who mindlessly pushed the timid gelding closer and closer to the gate. When the small horse was just about there, Dunne withdrew his hand, causing the stallion to snort in frustration.

The gate was shut with a length of bent fencing wire. As Dunne slowly twisted it open, the horses took a step or two back, though Dunne was thankful to see they were all farm stock and they did not run off or turn skittish. He shooed the stallion by pushing on its muzzle. He then held his hand out toward the gelding and in this way lured the smaller horse out of the enclosure. After loosely wiring the gate shut, he fed the horse the rest of the sugar and was happy when the horse wouldn't leave his side. Dunne then repeated the process to ensnare a second timid gelding, though it took longer this time, as the stallion was more persistent and wouldn't shoo when Dunne again opened the gate. When Dunne finally managed to lure the second gelding from the enclosure, his heart was beating hard, for it was almost nine o'clock in the morning and he was sure the ranch owners would have woken by then.

He thought about all the times he'd done this as a youth, and it was a thought that amused him.

"That's it," he kept saying as he led the two horses along the wagon ruts. "That's it ..."

The day was warm and sunny though there was a breeze, and in this breeze he could feel that autumn was coming. He led the horses up and over a knoll. When they were on the far side, he tied the rope to the second horse's bit. He then mounted the first horse and rode it along quiet country lanes with the second gelding in tow. As they rode, Dunne had to struggle to stay upright, for it had been a while since he had been on a horse and even longer since he had ridden one bareback. When ever one or both of the horses stopped to munch clover, he did not hurry them, nor did he bother to look around for approaching lawmen. He entered Chinatown and found a combination tack shop and auto garage run by a man who was willing to rent Dunne a pair of saddles for the day and, at the same time, not ask too many questions. When the horses were saddled, he thanked the man and paid him. He then rode in the direction of Sarah's house.

It was close to eleven in the morning, and it was his most fervent hope that he'd find her at home.

FIVE

SARAH MANN AWOKE MIDMORNING feeling shaky and cold. She rose and took a half-pill lifted from the hospital dispensary. When this didn't adequately control her symptoms, she took the other half and soon felt a warmth spread through her stomach that made her feel settled and whole and pleased.

"David," she called out, only to hear her voice issue first through the house and then her own mind, where the syllables echoed and slowly transmuted into the tapping of a wood block. Though she knew her brother wasn't home, she called his name again, just to hear the way her own voice burrowed inside her head and then turned into something musical and soft.

She was standing alone in her kitchen, newly transfixed by the prism of sunlight coming in through the window: it looked solid, like a shimmering column. She'd have to step around it if she didn't want to bruise her shin. This thought made her giggle, and the sound of her own amused voice reverberated inside her, this time turning into something birdlike and calling. She made tea and went into the garden.

The leaves on the oak trees lining her street were beginning to erupt with colour—gold, red, purple—and when she glanced from one tree to another, the colours streaked across her vision, forming kaleidoscopic bridges. This is what she liked about the hospital pills. Despite all the troubles that had befallen her and her brother, they made her stop worrying and feel happy and consider such things as hue and lightness and the feeling of her own bare feet against earth.

She looked around her glowing yard and suddenly realized that it was a mess. The grass was patchy and brown, there were weeds everywhere and the rose bushes planted near the boulevard were drooping and fringed with dark-green rot. She took a deep breath and asked herself how she'd let it get this far. Yes, there was a war on—no excuse, not really; in fact, in times of trouble it was even more important to make sure that the small things still got done. Sarah went back inside the house and searched through the clutter in her mudroom until she found an old trowel marred with rust spots and caked mud. She came back out and kneeled before the rose garden bed and began digging. Though she never had been much of a gardener—that had been her father's domain, and as such it did not interest her—she did know you had to get the tip of the trowel all the way beneath the rooting system so as to destroy the weed's chance of regeneration. She worked away. There were dandelions everywhere, some of which rubbed against her skin and turned the inside of her wrists a splotchy pink. She kept working away, the repetitiveness of the motion such that her thoughts wandered, and she began to think about the sergeant named Dunne.

She smiled.

She heard the far-off sound of hooves against packed roadway. When she looked up and saw him, a tiny bobbing image at the end of the street, she thought he must be a mirage, summoned by the thoughts travelling through her own looping mind. Yet as he rode toward her, a second horse trailing along behind, he grew larger and his face came into focus and the wrinkles in his clothing seemed real enough to touch.

He stopped on the street before her. Sarah stood, trying hard to disguise her wonderment.

"I know you don't take walks with soldiers," he said. "You think you could maybe take a ride with one instead?"

She began to grin and then stopped herself.

"I have a lunch," he added, and to illustrate he patted a saddlebag hanging off the near side of his horse.

"A good one?"

"Good enough."

"Would we be gone long?"

"We would."

She thought. She approached the horse beneath the sergeant.

"I probably shouldn't," she said while stroking the white, diamond-shaped spot between the animal's eyes. "He's beautiful, though."

THEY RODE THROUGH WILDFLOWER MEADOWS and wide grassy pastures and then they followed a mountain stream that undulated through a rift in the mountains. They rode slowly, and whenever Sarah's horse stopped to drink water or rest, Sergeant Dunne would stop and dismount and lead the horse toward his own, though if this didn't encourage the horse to move Dunne just waited until the animal grew restless and moved of his own accord. Above were hawks and eagles and a matting of sugar-white clouds. As the sun rose into the middle of the sky, it filled the chasm between the mountains and turned everything warm and yellow. Steam lifted from the surface of the creek, which began someplace far higher and ran with water that was refreshing to drink. Throughout, the two horses went at a pace of their own making. The sergeant said little except to comment on the occasional deer or buck rabbit, or the way in which an outcropping of rock reminded him of something. This didn't bother her; in this landscape, her life as a nurse and an orphan and a caretaker of a feckless younger brother seemed to belong to someone else, and this was a feeling that benefited her greatly.

Eventually, they emerged from the mountain pass and rode for another hour through a pasture of thistle and blue flowers and honeybees as big as a newborn's fist. They crossed over the top of a knoll and turned around a grove of birch and that's when she saw a ramshackle cabin turned to splinters through exposure to rain and neglect. The porch had come away from the front of the house and the stovepipe sticking through the rooftop was blackened with soot.

They stopped riding about twenty yards from the abandoned cabin. She looked over at the sergeant and saw something there akin to grim satisfaction.

"Sergeant," she said. "What are we doing here?"

"Wanted to show you where I grew up."

She looked at the cabin with new eyes. In so doing, she searched for things she liked about it other than the setting. "Can we go inside?" she asked.

"It's your choice," Dunne answered.

They hitched their horses to a rusting old pump protruding from the ground in front of the cabin.

"Careful," said Dunne as he stepped around holes in the collapsed veranda. He pushed open the door and she followed him into the gloom. She could make out newspapers and cardboard boxes chewed by mice and not much more. In one corner there was a woodstove and orange-stained basin.

With all of the dust and animal droppings it was difficult to breathe and she told him so. They stepped back into fresh air.

"It's not much," he said.

"You were poor."

"We were."

"When did you last live here?"

"A long time ago."

"What did your father do?"

"Came and went, mostly. He wasn't a big help."

"Your mother must have been tough."

"She was. It's something I've grown to dislike in women."

Sarah and Dunne walked away from the shack and stood in the full glare of sunshine. They looked not at each other but at the mountains in the distance, some of which were topped with snow.

"How do you know my name?" she asked.

"I asked around. It wasn't a challenge."

"You *are* a sergeant."

"Please," he said. "You think maybe you could call me Michael?"

She paused and thought this over and found the idea pleasing. "Only if I can ask you something."

"All right."

"Were you at Vimy?"

"I did attend that fight, yes."

"What was it like?"

Dunne's eyes narrowed and it looked to Sarah as though he was searching for something. "It was cold. In the end we took the ridge. Seems no one else could."

"At least you're home now."

"Yep," he said. "There's that."

They walked around the property. Behind the house Sarah noticed a clearing and in this clearing there was a cross made from two rough pieces of wood. As she approached, she saw that the cross had been fastened with long nails, the heads of which had turned orange with rust and bad weather. It protruded, waist level, from hard soil. On the horizontal beam were the words *Michael Dunne, 1880–1915.*

He came up behind her.

"Did you do that?" she asked.

"Was whisky did that."

She looked at him.

"When I enlisted, we were just starting to get the stories over here. I figured I was probably going to get killed in battle. Came pretty close to happening too."

"So then why'd you enlist in the first place?"

"Well now that's a story all by itself and maybe someday I'll tell it to you. C'mon. I've got something I want to show you."

Dunne unstrapped the saddlebag from his horse and led Sarah up a footpath that wound toward a nearby peak. Along the way they saw mule deer and several types of jay. The path circled around the summit of the peak, and they arrived upon the shore of a little lake that, in full daylight, looked as though it were surfaced with shimmering blue foil. There was a small pit enclosed by seating logs and in it Dunne lit a fire. He pulled out a coffee pot from his bag and filled it with grounds and water from a canteen. He then put it toward the edge of the fire, where the placement of two rocks formed a bridge for it to perch on. As they watched the coffee slowly come to a brew, they ate pork sandwiches and apples and they passed a small flask of whisky.

"You know," he said between bites. "Your brother tried to enlist yesterday."

Sarah sighed and thought, I'll kill him. I will. "What happened?"

"I didn't let him."

She peered at the sergeant, not understanding.

"I told him he was too damn young."

It came to her—an aching pull in the chest that foreshadows change in one's life, and an expansion of all things possible in that life. She gazed out over the lake and the mountains and the distant sky.

"Look at all this."

"I know."

"It's like a picture. Or a movie reel. It's like looking at something that isn't real. You just want to crawl into it forever."

Dunne reached out and took Sarah's hand; she did nothing to prevent it or to encourage more from happening. For the longest time they sat that way, touching fingers and saying nothing, and Sarah would have liked to stay that way forever, a million miles from war and wounded men, though as the sun began to arch toward the farther mountains the nerves in her fingertips began to burn and her scalp began to itch and she felt a mild upset come to her stomach. She glanced at Dunne and saw that his face was lined and rough and glowing pink in the strong, later-afternoon light.

"You know," she said. "This scene, the whole of it, seems at odds with the way I know the world to be."

"I know," he said, and suddenly the sense of change coming became so powerful she wished to be rid of it.

"I have to go now."

"I wish you didn't."

"I know."

They hiked back down to the horses and then rode back the same way they'd come, only this time their route seemed murky and foreboding and she wished only to be home. They reached her small house just after dusk, and by this time her hands were shaking and her forehead was damp and her stomach was cramping. As she walked toward her house, she heard his boot steps following along behind. At the door she turned.

"Thank you," she said.

"You're welcome."

"By the way. Where *did* you get those horses?"

"I borrowed them from a friend."

"You have a friend with horses?"

"I do. I gotta go return them."

She smiled and looked down. Though she understood that this was a stretching of the truth, she wasn't sure in what direction. She wished that her sergeant was a more talkative, flippant man—there was something about his comfort with silences that seemed to demand truthfulness or at least an approximation thereof.

"Michael," she finally said. "I'm flattered by this attention. I really am. But I don't think I can do this right now."

"I understand."

"It's just that things are very complicated for me."

"I know it. Fact is, I think maybe that's the attraction."

She smiled and said, "You're different, I'll give you that, Michael Dunne."

Without knowing what to do next, she leaned forward and kissed his cheek and, despite herself, let the kiss linger in a way that contradicted everything she'd just told him. She pulled away feeling weakened.

Michael Dunne straightened and said, only, "Good night, Sarah Mann."

He then turned and walked back to his likely stolen horses, and if Sarah wasn't mistaken the man was smiling.

SIX

DUNNE MOUNTED THE FIRST HORSE and retied the second and was about to return them to the paddock outside of town when he remembered that Royster mentioned something about staying at an address that was close. With the prospect of a long, sleepless night before him, Dunne ambled through the streets until he came to a house fashioned from tarpaper and ill-fitting shingles and when he spotted a wood block and axe in the yard something told him that it had to belong to Royster.

He knocked on the door. When Royster came,

he was unshaven and his stump was showing—
Dunne noticed it was mottled and round, a little
like the head of a turnip, and he tried not to look
at it.

"Get dressed," said Dunne, and when Royster
was ready they picked up another bottle at The Red
Letter and took the horses a short way out of town,
to a series of rolling foothills, each of which had a
view of the lights of the city. They picked one and
sat in darkness and because of the rum were not
conscious of the night's descending cold. The bottle
was still wrapped in brown paper and they passed
it back and forth.

"Christ," said Royster. "That's good. Burns a
little, though. Lot of rum over there, I guess."

"Yeah, but they water it down. Otherwise it
burns."

"Plentiful enough, though?"

"If there's a show on."

"A battle, you mean?"

Dunne nodded.

"Christ, that word's got a ring," said Royster.
"It's like, gotta be top of the world. And all the
shit the Boche get up to? They crucified one of
our guys, for God's sake. Right on a barn door, I
heard."

"Never happened. Great story, but it never happened."

"Still ..."

Royster lay on the ground and looked up at the sky and exhaled deeply.

"I follow it, you know. Lot of people, they could take it or leave it. But me? Every day come five o'clock I got the paper in my hand, nose right to the print. Every move you two make, you and Highway, I'm right on it. Jeez, I miss that old Indian. And this ain't just liquor talking, Mikey. Truth is, I'm proud as shit of you two. And I'll tell you something else, if it wasn't for this stump you know I'd be right between you and that old Sarcee on the firing line. Jeez, I miss that Indian. Yeah, I'd be right in the middle of it. That'd be me. Like I say, I'm proud of you, Mikey. And Highway."

"You don't need to be."

"Well I am."

"And I say you don't need to be."

They passed the bottle and didn't speak for a while.

"Royster," Dunne started.

"I'm right here."

"I killed a kid over there."

"A kid?"

"I killed others too, but there was a kid."

"A Kraut kid?"

"Course."

"Then so what?"

"Bothers me, is all. Makes everything here seem ... Jesus, what's the word? Immaterial? Is that it?"

"Dunno. It's your word."

"Makes everything here seem fake."

"Everything *is* fake, Mikey. I told you that a million times. Life's not worth getting worked up over."

Dunne laughed hoarsely, but then his voice cracked and he went silent. Royster took the bottle from his old friend.

"Mikey?"

"Yeah."

"You okay?"

"Sometimes I am. But I gotta say that sometimes I ain't."

"Guess that goes for a lot of people." Royster lifted his severed arm. "When you come right down to it, I guess that goes for me too."

"Listen," Dunne said. "I gotta go. That doctor named Walker is giving some presentation at the hospital tomorrow morning and for some reason I have to be there."

"What kinda presentation?"

"Some training thing. He'll be talking about wartime medicine. A doctor who's never been to war talking to doctors who'll never go either."

"You hate him."

"Not him specifically, but men like him."

The two friends stood and drained the last of the bottle so that when they rode back to Royster's it was all they could do to stay on their respective horses. They dropped the saddles in a safe place behind the Chinaman's, and by the time Dunne snuck the horses back into the paddock—he doubted the owner had noticed they were gone—it was the dead of night and he could hear the call of owls and coydogs as he stumbled toward town. He made it to his rooming house, the far end of the city starting to turn a pale, husky lavender. He fumbled with his key and then, upon entering the house, accidentally toppled an umbrella stand; he froze, listening intently, for it had recently occurred to him that his landlady really would throw him out if he caused any more problems. And with all the young men returning with missing limbs and damaged minds she'd have no trouble finding another wreck to take his spot.

He heard nothing and he crept up to his room. He lay in his clothes and thought of Sarah and the boy he'd killed and the possible reasons why the two thoughts always seemed to come to him in tandem. It was as though there were a scale in his head, and the two sides were somehow balanced by Sarah on one side and the boy on the other, and if this scale ever went out of balance there'd be hell to pay. He slept intermittently for the next two hours and then got up feeling far worse than before he'd slept—his stomach was gurgling and his head was still swimming with rum. He stayed in the shower for a good long time, until one of the other roomers started banging on the door and yelling something that Dunne couldn't hear over the rain of water.

In his room he dressed in his military uniform; he left with a pounding head and a queasy stomach. He drank coffee after coffee in a local diner, where he sat at a counter between two mineral prospectors who did little but stare ahead while glumly chewing. Then he walked to the city's main hospital, which was three blocks away from the makeshift hospital where he'd been treated for shell shock.

The lecture hall was a large, wood-panelled room filled with people. As instructed, he found his way to a desk before the lectern, in front of an assembly of physicians; as he walked toward his seat, he scanned the crowd and noticed that Sarah was there, and when he caught her eye she smiled weakly and then looked into her lap. Suddenly, he felt okay.

Major Dobson-Hughes was seated at the table as well, and as the crowd calmed itself he leaned over to Dunne and said, "You're bloody well late."

"I am."

"Inexcusable."

"Was my neurasthenia slowed me down, sir."

Dobson-Hughes reddened and glared at Dunne and would likely have chastened the sergeant further had the day's speaker not entered the front of the lecture hall. There was polite applause, which Dr. Walker dimmed by raising his hands. Behind him was an easel covered with a piece of tan cloth; he flipped it over the board to reveal an enlarged photograph of a battlefield wound. The hall was silent now.

"The soldier in the modern battlefield is beset with many challenges."

Dr. Walker indicated the photograph and paced for effect.

"Most notable among them is artillery. Tissue damage results from the fragments that are irregular in shape. In the soft parts, wounds show deep and extensive attritions and are marked by an effusion of the blood and/or serum."

Again, he paused to look at the audience. Many were taking notes.

"Wounds are typically jagged or, at best, unpredictable. Invariably, shell fragments will introduce foreign matter into the wound, making infection inevitable. Are there any questions so far?"

He scanned the audience, saw no hands and continued.

"Contused wounds typically are vast erosions, big furrows, large lesions forming a sort of cul-de-sac. More like wounds with large pieces of tissue hanging from them, fimbriated, ecchymotic in their depths ... abrasions with torn surfaces and herniated muscles. Artillery shells will splinter, amputate, decapitate, bisect, quarter or otherwise grossly mutilate the human frame."

As Dr. Walker spoke, Dunne drifted off; the sight of Sarah had made him think about yesterday, about their ride through the mountains and their talk by sunlit water. He thought about how much he'd enjoyed the day and how good his lunch had tasted and then, for reasons he did not understand, he suddenly felt guilty and found himself thinking of the boy he'd speared in the church pulpit. Probably, he thought, it was wrong for someone like him to dare loving.

Dr. Walker was still talking.

"Shell blasts can create vacuums in the body's organs, rupturing lungs and producing hemorrhages in the brain and spinal cord. In other words, death by concussion. An unmarked body on the exterior, and utter destruction on the interior. In the worst of cases, a direct explosion will obliterate the man. The soldier will simply disappear. Thank you."

There was polite applause. Dunne turned and looked for Sarah and he saw that she, too, was applauding and that she wore thin white gloves on her finely boned hands.

"Today, we have with us Sergeant Michael Dunne. Sergeant Dunne is a Calgary native, I'm told, and has received a decoration for his service in battle. He is currently employed in recruitment services. Sergeant Dunne …"

Dr. Walker motioned for Dunne to stand and when he did so there was more polite applause.

"Thank you for being with us today."

Dunne nodded.

"Tell us, Sergeant Dunne. Is there anything you can think to add to this subject?"

"I beg your pardon?"

"I am asking if you can think of anything I may have overlooked."

"No, that's pretty much what happens."

"So you would agree that artillery represents the greatest challenge to an individual in the battlefield?"

Dunne felt ill, all over, as though afflicted with a poison he had no choice but to eject. He narrowed his eyes, and though he knew he shouldn't say what was running through his head he said it anyway.

"No sir. I wish I did, but I don't. The greatest challenge to a soldier in the battlefield is trying to keep his matches dry."

There was laughter, though it died immediately when the gathered physicians noticed the expression on the lecturer's face. For the next several moments, there was a silence that, to Dunne, felt treacherously close to the experience of joy.

WHEN THE LECTURE WAS OVER and the assembly dismissed, Dobson-Hughes grabbed Dunne by the arm and led him out of the hall via an exit at the front. He released him only when they reached an alley leading to Centre Street. They walked in silence, Dobson-Hughes a half-step ahead of Dunne, and when they reached the recruitment headquarters Dobson-Hughes proceeded straight to his office. When he realized that Dunne was no longer behind him, he turned in the doorway and puffed up his chest and said, "Your presence *is* required, sergeant."

Dunne hesitated for a moment and then followed Dobson-Hughes into his office.

"Sit."

Dunne took the chair opposite his boss's desk and watched as the man paced back and forth.

Eventually he stopped and rested his knuckles on the desktop and glared at Dunne.

"Keeping your matches dry."

"Yes sir."

"Never have I heard such insolence. Never have I heard such cheek. *Keeping your matches dry.* Jesus, man, what were you thinking? Dr. Walker is one of the foremost clinicians in this city. With that single comment you turned his entire lecture into a farce."

"It was a goddamn farce to begin with."

"Oh it was, was it?"

"Walker doesn't know a thing."

"And how's that?"

"He's never been to battle."

"Well I *have*."

"Then you should know."

"Sergeant Dunne. You had a diagnosis, did you not?"

"I did."

"And I think we both know what it means."

Dunne glared and said nothing.

"You're an embarrassment, sergeant. You and I both know it. I've been keeping close eyes on you and the company you keep."

"The company I keep?"

"A certain one-armed sawmill worker."

"He's got nothing to do with me."

"How about a certain nurse with a questionable family history?"

Dunne felt his eyes narrow and his insides turn to stone. He took a slow deep breath to show that he was neither unnerved nor anything close to it. "I'm no man for puzzles, major. You got something to say I suggest you say it."

"Are you threatening me, Dunne?"

"I'm just saying what is."

A few poisonous moments passed between them. Suddenly, Dobson-Hughes grinned, and Dunne knew that this was meant to keep him off balance.

"Listen to me," said the major. "No point in either one of us saying something we might regret later on. No point in you and I getting into the *real* muck of it. I can see you are taxed. I can see you need a rest. Why don't you take a few days off? Relax, and try not to spend too much time in the saloons, what? I'll let you know when to report back for duty. Fresh air and sunshine would do you some good."

Dunne said nothing and stood and strode out of the office. He spent the next few days carousing with bad people and several times he walked over to Sarah's house, where he hoped he'd catch her coming in or out, at which time he planned to feign an accidental meeting. On the third day, his landlady finally had enough of his comings and goings and she told him that, war hero or not, he had to go and he had to go now. He left and did not feel bad doing so.

Her rooming house stood at the outskirts of a section of town that respectable people avoided; to look for a new place to stay, Dunne instinctively burrowed deeper into that world. It took him less than an hour. His new rooming house was cheaper and run by an old Greek and there were exotic smells in the dank hallways and though his room was not untouched by vermin it didn't bother him for he did not feel he deserved better. It was just three doors over from The Red Letter and at all hours of the day or night he could lie in his bed and listen to the sound of laughter and talking and arguments settled by gunshot.

He thought constantly of Sarah.

He'd left his new address with his ex-landlady. On his sixth day of leave, Dunne came home and found a small envelope on the dusty floor, about two inches inside his room. He bent over and, knowing exactly what it was, picked it up. He opened it. It was written by Carmichael, the other clerk at the recruitment office, and it read:

> *Please be informed that Sergeant Michael Dunne is due to report to the*

*10th Battalion Recruitment Office at
0800 hours tomorrow morning.*

That night, in an attempt to make amends, he
got a haircut and he had his shoes shined by a dwarf
who ran a stand on the corner. He reported on time,
which was not normally his practice, as there was
little to do in the hour before they started seeing
volunteers at nine. To pass the time, he drank coffee and read the newspaper and chatted with Carmichael, who looked glad to have Dunne back. At
nine, he started seeing recruits, though he no longer
asked them if they minded muddy conditions or
getting shot at—to appease Dobson-Hughes (who
didn't seem to be around that day), he just asked
them the required questions and sent them for their
medical unless they were truly too old or crippled
or degenerate.

Around midmorning, a rickety old man
approached him. In his hands he carried a rolled-
up sheet of some sort, which he proceeded to
unroll on Dunne's station.

"What is it?" asked Dunne.

"Mechanical drawings."

"I think you're in the wrong place, old-timer."

The old man acted as though he didn't hear
him. "They're plans for a machine."

"A machine?"

"Yep. Have a look."

"I am."

A panicked expression suddenly crossed the old man's face. He reached down and rotated the plans, which even Dunne could see were a nonsensical arrangement of lines and numbers.

"Sorry," said the old-timer. "I had it upside down."

"Ahhh!" Dunne said. "Now it makes sense."

"Like I say, it's a machine."

"Of course it is."

"You'll notice I've left out certain mechanical secrets that can only be revealed upon payment of one million dollars."

"That's a nice round figure. But forgive my ignorance. What exactly will this invention of yours accomplish?"

"It will bring the war to an end in forty-eight hours."

"Well now that's something worth pursuing. How exactly will it do that?"

"With this machine, an individual can circle the globe in exactly fifteen minutes."

"That's fast."

"Think of what you could do."

Dunne looked up and saw what he should have seen from the first: the old man was a sad reminder that soldiers and their widows weren't the only ones driven mad during wartime. Dunne sighed and stood. He took the old man by the elbow and took him to a kitchenette that Carmichael kept near the rear of the office. Here he offered the old man a cup of coffee.

"Your plans are good, chief. We'll be in touch. In the meantime, don't show them to anyone else."

"I won't."

"And if you want to come back and show them to me again you just do that. Coffee's always on, here."

"I will, sergeant. I surely will."

Dunne showed the old man to the street and watched him walk away beaming. After taking a little bit of sun and cool air, he returned to his station and saw to a couple of other questionable recruits before he noticed the major come striding in. He marched into his office and shut the door and a minute later poked his head out. When he caught Dunne's eye, he motioned that he should come.

Dunne went to the major's office and sat.

"Sergeant Dunne," Dobson-Hughes started. "The ground on which we are standing is shifting. Civilization hangs in the balance, and when something like this comes to my attention it is my duty to offer a word of warning. You are plowing a foreign field."

Dunne looked at him blankly. "This got something to do with matches, sir?"

"We are talking about Sarah Mann."

"She's got nothing to do with any problem you and I have."

"Oh it's much bigger than you and I, sergeant. More specifically, we are talking about her father."

"He fought at Vimy. Same ridge I fought at. Only difference is I lived and he didn't."

"The only difference you're *aware* of, what?"

It was then Dunne noted that a single file rested on the major's desk. Dobson-Hughes sat and put on reading glasses and began reading aloud. In that instant, his voice turned icy, and Dunne felt as though he was seeing the major for the man he really was.

"Martin Mann was born in Ingolstadt, Bavaria."

"So he was born in Germany. You know how many German settlers came to these parts?"

"Herr Mann returned to his native land in 1915 and was assigned to the 2nd Bavarian Regiment. Sergeant, he fought for the enemy. Your lady friend's father was the enemy."

Dunne said nothing. Dobson-Hughes lowered his voice. "The blood is tainted, sergeant. Ottawa mandates that we must root out the Hun in sheep's clothing and root him out we will. Oh yes, we will. Like a pig, if we have to."

SEVEN

S ARAH SLEPT IN THE BED in which her parents
once slept. It was a place alive with old scents
and memories and the lure of time long since
passed, and when she dreamt her visions were
warm and sepia-toned, as if occurring in a resur-
rected movie reel. She ordinarily slept till midday,
unaffected by the noise coming from the street and
the daylight creeping around her blinds and the
stomping of her younger brother, who made his
breakfast with all the delicacy of a town drunk.
Her dreams were a blaze of hot colour, unbur-
dened by lost parents or a grizzled sergeant with

whom she may or may not have fallen in love. She slept heavily, her breathing barely perceptible, her heartbeat slowed and heavy. She slept with her hands atop her bedspread. She slept with her soul transported. She slept, motionlessly, lost to a morphine stillness, her aging stalled, with no sense of time's passage, so that when she did wake, after ten straight hours, she often felt as though she had been asleep for one second and one second only, and she would lie in the shaded gloom of the bedroom, worrying she might never return to such a blissful state.

She slept, she did, until the louts outside wakened her.

At first she wondered at the cause for those heckling male voices. They sounded drunk, she thought, and for this reason their voices—so rough, so indecent—pierced the usual clamour in the street. She sat and rubbed her face and commanded herself awake, a task she always found difficult. Today, having planned to sleep to the middle of the afternoon, she found it impossible. She yawned and teetered over onto her side and still their voices—it was though they were chanting something—prevented her from falling back asleep. She thought of taking another pill though she knew she shouldn't, she was trying to cut down, she already had enough of a problem.

She got out of bed. The bottom inch or two of her bedroom window was not covered by the ill-fitting curtain; through it, she could see sunlight and dust rising and for some reason she viewed this as a sorrowful omen.

Sarah put on an old dress and shoes. When she moved into the kitchen, which faced onto the street, the voices became louder, and she could now hear that they were saying a single word, over and over, a single hard-punching syllable, something starting with an *H*.

Something, she thought, with the intention to wound.

Instead of making strong coffee she moved to the kitchen window and peered out and she saw them, big-armed farmboys with poor haircuts and tattoos, passing around a flask, probably grain alcohol or maybe something worse, and in her fog she still couldn't fathom why they were there or why they were pumping their fists in the air or why they were saying that word over and over again.

She listened, more intently, until the ear-chatter caused by opiates and dream residue faded, and she could make out what they were saying. She bent over the sink and put her face in her hands and started to weep, for it had always been her worst fear that her father's actions would be uncovered.

Hun … Hun … Hun … Hun …

... and when she finally stood she called out her brother's name though of course he wasn't home, he was never home, and she wondered whether the louts had been there when he left for the newspaper office that morning. Probably not, she thought, that was *his* sort of luck, and when she went outside and told them to leave her alone they laughed and chanted louder and took menacing steps toward her so she turned back into the house and shut all the doors. She raced to her room and hid, covers pulled high over her head, and they were there for hours, it seemed, for days and weeks and months, until finally she noticed that the chanting faded and was replaced by drunken chatter and then the chatter was gone altogether.

She rose, her cheeks traced with dried salt.

Damn you, Papa, she thought. Damn you.

SHE WENT TO THE KITCHEN to start her day. She brewed strong coffee and made toast, though when she went to eat it her throat was constricted and everything within her felt sour.

A girl from the hospital came to the house. She couldn't have been any older than fifteen, a local schoolkid volunteering for the cause. Sarah was looking out the window when she turned onto the front path. Suddenly, the girl stopped and, for a moment, looked alarmed before dropping her head and continuing to the stoop. Sarah heard her knock on the door.

Sarah opened it just an inch.

"Sarah Mann?" the girl peeped.

She was pretty and small and she had big brown eyes and, in that second, Sarah hated them for making her do this.

"I'm Sarah."

"They want you to come to the hospital."

"Do I put on my uniform?"

"They said you didn't have to."

"No," Sarah said. "I guess I wouldn't have to."

The girl blinked and looked uncomfortable. Sarah felt bad for her.

"Tell them I'll get there when I get there."

She went back inside and was in no hurry to finish her coffee. When she finally did, she sat at her kitchen table for the longest time, pretending that none of this was happening and that none of the things in the cramped room where she sat had anything to do with her.

She rose and left; when she turned to look back at the house where she had grown up, she saw that the words *Bloody Hun* had been scrawled across the front siding in towering red letters. She swallowed hard, and as she walked down the street she was conscious of curtains parting and eyes peering out. She reached the hospital and there she was greeted by her boss, a bastard named Fitzgerald, and the major from the recruitment office, the one with the bushy moustache and the stiff accent. She was led into Fitzgerald's office and told to sit. Fitzgerald sat beside his desk while Major Dobson-Hughes paced. There was also a uniformed police officer, standing silent near the window.

"I'm fired," she said.

Her frankness surprised them and for several moments none of the men spoke.

"I'm sorry, Miss Mann," said Fitzgerald. "Our mandate is uncompromising. Our regrets."

"You regret nothing," she said. "The least you could do is afford me the courtesy of being honest. Is there anything in my record to justify this?"

"No," said Fitzgerald. "Admittedly, you have been a dutiful employee."

"So I'm to be dismissed for no other reason than I have German blood?"

"German blood? Your father fought for the enemy, Sarah."

Dobson-Hughes spoke. "I shouldn't expect a

woman to understand this, but our country is rife with saboteurs."

"Oh for God's sake. When did nursing wounded soldiers become a threat to the homeland? And if I'm so dangerous why don't you lock me up?"

"At this moment, internment is not under consideration."

Sarah looked right at Dobson-Hughes. "And you have been living in this country ... for how long exactly?"

"That is none of your business."

"I've been living here my whole life!"

"There's no cause for hysteria," Fitzgerald interjected.

"I'm not hysterical. I'm Canadian."

"It doesn't matter," said Dobson-Hughes. "*I* was born under the sun of the British Empire. You, Miss Mann, were born under the cloud of Germany. You should be thankful we don't arrest you and have you placed in a camp for hostile Germans."

.

SARAH TRUDGED HOME feeling the beginnings of her sickness. She reached her house and when she saw that more paint had been thrown on it a pain sizzled through her bones and her veins and her muscles. David was in the kitchen.

"What are you doing?"

"Sitting at a table and looking at the floor."

She joined him. "Why aren't you at work?"

He looked at her balefully and then let his eyes drop back to the floor and she knew he'd lost his job as well.

"We could move," she said. "Start over. We could find other work."

"Doing what?"

"Many things."

"Not in this city."

"No. Not here."

"Who'd buy this house? Look at what they've done to it. We'd be starting with nothing."

Sarah didn't answer and for the longest time they didn't speak.

"Do you hate him?" she finally asked.

"Our father?"

"Seems every serious conversation we have leads to him."

"I do," said David.

"He never fit in here. It made him vengeful and mean."

"I always figured it was the other way around."

"You could be right."

"He drove Ma into an early grave. I'm sure of it."

"I'm sure of it too."

David stood and went to his room; she heard drawers opening and closing and the sound of his muttering sharp voice. Fatigue and joint pain gnawed at her. The nerves in her scalp and fingertips flamed and she was possessed with a desire to hurt herself. She stood and made it to her room and pulled out a little mother-of-pearl box she kept in the back of the bottom dresser drawer. The box, which was originally intended for earrings or perhaps a small necklace, had once belonged to her mother; it had often occurred to Sarah that perhaps it was not a coincidence that she now used it to keep the most precious thing in her life.

She flipped open the top and shuddered; there were only three morphine tablets, looking chalky and blue and forlorn. She had meant to steal more on her next shift, and the fact that her life had come to this—thieving from the hospital dispensary, taking what belonged in the mouths of wounded soldiers, her life planned out from pill to pill—sickened her more than her withdrawal symptoms. Even if she took halves, which would barely control her cravings, she'd be fine for a day or two at the most, and then it would start all over again, the restless planning and scheming and worry.

Carefully, she broke one in half and lamented the tiny grains that went flying in the process.

She swallowed the half and waited and over the next half-hour felt only the mildest effect. She was frantic with worry now. She heard her front door slam and when she weakly called for David there came no answer. From inside the house, she watched the louts assemble outside once again. It even sounded like there might be more of them this time, and she thought it strange how much they'd bothered her before, and how she now considered them way, way down on her list of problems.

Sarah went to her room and lay down and looked at the ceiling and felt a dull ache possess her muscles. She was crying. She had one wish only and when she heard a hesitant knocking on her door she wondered if God had heard her and issued forgiveness for all the things she'd done to displease Him.

EIGHT

H E SAW THEM FROM A DISTANCE, three beefy rubes passing a flask and jeering, and when he neared he could see what had been done to Sarah's house and in that instant he decided he would take her away from there. The young men—they might as well have had hay sticking to their backs—were laughing and gesturing and intermittently yelling, "Come on out, you fucking Hun bitch," and, "You can't hide forever, you goddamn Boche whore."

Dunne passed them and they quieted momentarily when they saw that he was heading up her walkway. He knocked on her door. When she answered, the sight of her peering out of the slightly opened door inspired more slurs and called-out vulgarities. Her eyes were red, Dunne could see, and she was chewing her lower lip.

"Nice neighbours," he said, and she opened the door just wide enough for him to step inside. The kitchen was at the front of the house, and Sarah walked over to the counter and leaned on it. She kept her back to him, and Dunne understood that her main torment at that moment was shame.

"Are you okay?"

She didn't answer.

"Where's David?"

"I don't know. Cassie's, maybe. Or maybe our mother's grave. He does that sometimes."

Dunne walked to the window and saw that another lout had shown up outside. He wished he could put his arms around her.

"You can't stay here."

"The thought had occurred to me."

"You can use my place. Go out the back. We'll meet up at my room. It's 213 Orr Street, number four."

"They'll see me," she said, for the first time nodding in the direction of the angered young men on the street.

"They won't. They'll be busy with something else."

There was a long pause, during which Sarah appeared to grow exhausted and pale.

"Sergeant? Why are you helping me?"

"I was on that ridge where your father died. It could've been me who killed him. Probably wasn't, but it could've been."

She looked at him through brimming eyes. "That's it?"

"It is."

"I don't believe you," she said before grabbing her coat and slipping out of the back door of her house.

DUNNE EXITED THROUGH THE FRONT DOOR and headed toward the goon who seemed to be the drunkest and the mouthiest and in charge of the others. He was big and blond and had tattoos on his forearms that either he or his dull, thick-necked buddies had done themselves; Dunne had seen a thousand others just like them. He took a deep breath and, a yard or two away, smiled.

"Hey sport!" he called out, beaming like a

child, and when the guy said, "What?" Dunne summoned every vestige of pain and outrage living within him and he used it to smash his forehead into the bridge of the farmboy's nose. Immediately, he knew he'd used too much force as there was the sound of small bones crunching, and the pain exploding through Dunne's own forehead made him feel alive and glorious and real. The farmboy fell and Dunne was on top of him, punching him again and again in the side of the face while the others slowly backed away. When he was finally done, his knuckles were sticky and red, and his shirt was damp with blood flowing from the cut on his forehead, and he screamed, "You touch one hair on her head, you're dead," although he wasn't at all sure if the farmboy could hear him. Though he was still breathing—Dunne could see his rib cage rise and fall—he wasn't in any way moving.

He stood and wiped blood from his eyes and slowly lit a cigarette as the others continued backing away slowly. He was breathing hard. His hair had fallen over his forehead and he could feel that some of it was sticking into his wound. The farmboy at his feet started to writhe and moan, just a little, and there was a part of Dunne that felt relieved and a part of Dunne that still wanted to finish the job.

Then and only then did he look at the other three.

"What're you looking at?" and when none of them answered he inhaled deeply on his cigarette and passed through them, making sure his right shoulder bumped hard against one of their shoulders as he did. He went home, thankful he was staying in a neighbourhood in which a bleeding man could walk down the street and nothing would happen save a few Chinamen turning to take a quick, curious look.

She was waiting for him on the stoop of his rooming house. When she saw him her eyes widened and her hand covered her mouth. She rose and went to him, though she stopped short of touching him.

"It's nothing," he said.

He fished his keys out of his pocket with hands still shaking from adrenalin and release. She slipped past him into his room. As soon as she entered, he went to the bathroom and wiped at the cut with a damp cloth; it wasn't deep but, being so close to the scalp, had bled more than it had a right to. For the next ten minutes he cleaned it and bandaged it as well as he could and then he joined Sarah.

She was looking around the room. Dunne knew what she was thinking.

"You can have the bed."

She sat on the edge of the mattress and looked downward.

"Sergeant, I ..."

"Please. Michael."

"Michael," she said, the name still unnatural on her lips. "There's another problem. A worse one."

"I know about that, yes."

She flitted her gaze toward him. When he saw that her eyes were full of remorse and embarrassment, he couldn't help but confront the notion that he loved her more than he had ever loved anyone or anything.

"I know about that," he said again.

"You saw me," she said. "At the hospital."

"I saw everything you did, Sarah."

"I don't take it every day," she lied.

"If you say so."

"I had trouble sleeping ... there was so much of it at the hospital, nobody ever counted it, there was so, so much of it ... it seemed like it was no big deal at first."

"You don't have to explain. It's the same at the front. There are more there who're like you than not. Sometimes I think this whole war runs on morphine. Sometimes I think if they took the morphine away, everyone would realize what they'd been doing and they'd walk away from the trenches, shocked and full of hate for themselves."

Dunne's room was quiet and still.

"I'm going to get sick," she said.

"Yes," he said. "You are."

IT STARTED WITH A TINGLING in her fingertips that
quickly turned to a smarting burn. The heat then
spread, like a flaming stream, through her veins and
arteries and though this hurt, it was *feeling* the flow
of hot blood through her body that made her whim-
per. She trembled and, despite the fire in her veins,
broke into feverish chills. Later, the burning in her
veins attacked her muscles, though when it did the
sensation of extreme heat turned into a fierce, flu-
like ache and when this happened she was visited
with images of her father, of her ranting, tyrannical,
browbeating father, floating through the room, hec-
toring and accusing, and it didn't matter which way
she turned he was always there, cast in a spectral
violet, jeering.

Whenever she vomited, Dunne carried away
her bedpan. When her sweats became bad, he
put cold compresses on her forehead and told her
everything was going to be all right. At one point
she called out to him and asked him to hold her,
but when he did the skin on his hands felt like
sandpaper and the fibres of his shirt like barbed
wire and she pushed him away, crying, "No no

no." This went on for an hour and then by her own recollection she was cast into some hellish neverland in which ghouls and twin-headed demons ran through her dreams, even when her eyes opened. This was the part that was too much; she sprang from Dunne's bed and raced to the door, thinking she could break into the hospital if that's what it took, only to have Dunne grab her and drag her, pleading, back to bed, which was now damp to the mattress with acrid, white-staining sweat.

A little later she became convinced that Dunne was some gargoyle-faced version of her father, and she began panicking and she slapped at him, and if Dunne hadn't been a strong man and a patient man she might have run through the streets wailing. Instead, she was pinned, the monster having grabbed her wrists and held them to either side of her head. And though it was true he was saying quiet, consoling words, she knew they were meant only to trick her into submission at which point (there wasn't a doubt in her mind) the monster would pick at her flesh with talons long and ghoulish. The walls of the room were purple and turned waxy by the flames licking from her own tortured body, and as it went on and on the ceiling flashed with forked lightning.

And then, as though a switch had been thrown, the room returned to normal and it was just

Dunne sitting in the chair next to her. She was still sweating badly, and now she saw her mother in the room with her, sitting on the side of her bed, stroking her hair and saying, *You're a young girl, Sarah, you are. You've your whole world ahead of you. There's no reason to be worried or frightened*, and it was the kindness of these words that made Sarah extremely sad, and appreciative that the mercy generated by the world can sometimes be the thing that kills you. She cried, then, for it all seemed so pointless, and she wasn't sure whether it was Michael Dunne or Astrid Mann who told her that it was all right, that she was safe, that soon it would all be over.

Sarah slept for twelve straight hours, and though her dreams were feverish and she awoke in soaked bedclothes, she nonetheless felt ready for a mug of hot broth.

Then she remembered. Michael Dunne—he had been there for all of it. This thought caused another wave of despondency to wash over Sarah, for she had dim memories of a vile, multicoloured torrent coming out of her, like something issued from hell, and she could only think that it was Dunne who had cleaned her up and for this reason she felt humiliated.

Plus, he was gone. She had driven him away with her sickness. He had said he'd known what to expect, though in the end he hadn't ... how could he have? ... and so, disgusted and fed up and hating this weak, snivelling thing she was, he left for good and this thought made her eyes redden and her stomach feel upset all over again.

Dunne entered the room with a fresh damp cloth and a tired way about him. He put it on her forehead and its coolness made her feel better.

"Thank you," she said.

"You're welcome."

"I've never felt more embarrassed."

"No need. So you got yourself in trouble. It's what people do."

She looked down and wondered whether this feeling of shame would ever leave her.

"We all have a curse," he said. "You're lucky. Yours is more common than some. Least with yours, it's easy to put a name to it."

He warmed soup on a hot plate and gave it to her. After that, she slept, more soundly this time. When she awoke she felt less like some key part of her was dying.

"I need a shower."

"You do."

It was close to four o'clock in the morning. He gave her a robe and a bar of soap and told her where the bathroom was.

"I'll go for a walk," he said.

"You don't have to."

"I'll give you some privacy. Be careful in the halls. And don't shower for too long or the hot water will go."

He turned and was out the door and she wondered whether there were places open at this hour for men like Michael Dunne. She padded down the barely lit hallway, and as she did the floorboards beneath her feet made a sound like heavy twigs rustling. Every part of her felt shaky and uncomfortable, as if run through with a low voltage of electricity; when she saw a large mouse look at her and then scurry into a baseboard fissure, her heart sped and she felt weak all over and she understood that for the rest of her life she would crave the jellied, distant feeling caused by hospital tablets.

The water ran cold for the longest time. Finally, it turned warm, and then close to hot; the room filled with steam and the sound of water drumming against tile. She let the water run over her face and trickle down her throat and feel hot in her stomach. As the cascade fell on her closed eyes, it made small bursts of red light against her retinas and for the longest time she watched these as though they were stars. The water turned cool and then cold; Sarah stepped out and dried herself and went back to Dunne's room, where she once again went to sleep.

She awoke with a dry mouth and the sense that her skin had dried to the consistency of old paper. Dunne was sitting in the chair beside her. He looked tired. She sat up and tried to neaten her hair.

"How long have I been in this room?" she asked.

"Two days. A bit more."

"Why aren't you at work?"

"I'm sick today."

"Do they know that?"

"They'll figure it out. I'll probably be sick tomorrow as well. I have egg sandwiches and coffee."

He handed her a wax-paper package and a hot paper cup. She ate because she knew she should, though the eggs tasted pasty and the coffee like hot tar and both seemed to leave a harsh, metallic taste on her tongue. She wondered if the taste of food would be this way from now on.

"Michael Dunne," she said. "If there were pills here I'd take them. I'd try not to, but I would."

Dunne shrugged. "The things that hurt us are generally the things we can't help yearning for. Leastways with most people I know."

"Can I ask you something?"

"You can."

"What did you do before being a soldier?"

"Most things. The sawmills. A mine or two out east. I was a farmhand in Saskatchewan. I even did rodeo for awhile and if you've ever wondered why my collarbone's a little crooked that's the reason why."

"Ever been married?"

"Once. In Victoria. I couldn't stand the nice weather. It didn't work out and that's part of the reason I ended up in the army."

"I don't understand."

She watched as he shifted in his chair.

"I somehow ended up in Fort Macleod, jobless and feeling sorry for myself and on the tail end of a three-day tear. When loneliness and liquor gang up on each other, the results are usually less than pretty."

"Something bad happened."

"It did. Me and a wrangler I'd spent the afternoon drinking with stumbled into the Confederation Bank and drew a pair of pistols. Demanded all of their money and didn't get a cent. My buddy got himself shot, though when they fired back at me I was already out the door. Thing was, we'd been stupid and careless and I knew they'd got a good look at me. I *knew* it was only a matter of time before they put a name to a face."

"So what did you do?"

"That night I ran. Kept mostly to fields and dirt roads. Kept running. I made it to Calgary hungry and worn and I figured the one place they wouldn't find me was Europe. I enlisted and hid out at the homestead until ship-out day."

"It was then you carved your grave."

"Stupid."

Sarah looked at him and surprised herself by laughing out loud. "And then they promoted you to sergeant!"

Dunne smiled and when he did the lines radiating from his eyes deepened and gave him an air of sorrowful wisdom. "I didn't even want the promotion, but they told me it'd be insubordinate not to take it. Seems I have personality traits befitting the rigours of battle. A captain told me that more than once. Maybe he was even right."

They both laughed quietly and then Dunne became solemn.

"This war's the worst thing that's ever happened to me. I did unspeakable things over there."

"Other soldiers have told me the same."

"This one's telling you the truth. Strange thing is, it makes me think about going back. Strange thing is, I look at you and there's a part of me still thinking about going back."

Sarah looked at him and wished to kiss him but,

at the same time, could think only of the way in which he'd seen her the last two days. "Well, you aren't going back. They wouldn't let you. But if you did I'd want you to follow one rule."

"What's that?"

"Don't die."

"It's not my desire to do so." Dunne paused. "Or leastways it's not one I know about."

NINE

ARLIER THAT LONG NIGHT, a night in which the moon was a wizened sliver and the sky was alive with bats and small owls, David caught a ride with a cooper pulling a wagon full of barrels. In his pocket he had three months' worth of good wages, which he'd taken from a jar he kept in the back of his closet. He was let off downtown and he walked past tall, silent buildings to Cassie's neighbourhood. Unlike the place where he lived with his sister, at this hour everything fell quiet, and when he stood looking at Cassie's dark, turreted home it seemed that the only sounds he could hear were the ones produced by his own spooling mind. It had been two days since he'd lost his job, two days spent deciding what to say to Cassie.

He looked up and admired the fullness of that night's Orion. He walked up the path toward the front of the house; right where the path met the steps leading to the grand stone porch, he turned to the left. His feet and pant cuffs dampened as he walked through wet, freshly mowed grass toward the side of the house. Once he reached Cassie's second-storey window he stood beneath it and, as he'd done so many times in the past, picked up a handful of pebbles from a shrub bed.

He took a deep breath and threw the pebbles toward the window; they struck with a light pattering and then fell back around his wet feet. When there was no reaction, he picked up a handful of small stones and threw them up at the window and when her light still didn't come on he whispered loudly, "*Cassie.*"

He listened. He heard the rustling of wind in conifer trees and a dog barking somewhere far off and that was all.

"Cassie," he called again, and this time when her light came on his heart soared, it being his opinion that no matter how difficult and stupid things were it didn't matter so long as he had Cassie. Looking up, he saw the curtains part, and her pretty face was backlit by the soft light of the room, and he called her name again: "Cassie, Cassie, it's David." All he could do was stand there in wonder, for her hair cascaded over one shoulder and her nightie was loose enough that he could see a hollow of revealed skin, right where the base of her neck met the top of her chest, though in the light thrown by the oil lamp her alabaster skin looked orange and flickering and alive.

He then noticed she wasn't smiling.

"Open the window," he hissed, and still she looked down at him, neither frowning nor smiling, and that was when he saw it: a slight shake of her head. And then she closed the curtain and a second later the room again went dark.

"Cassie!" he yelled, no longer caring who could hear him. "Cassie, it's me, goddamn it!" and when no response came other than the unremitting darkness of her window, he yelled her name again, this time in a voice turned gruff and desperate, for there was not one part of him that could accept what was occurring. He marched back to the front of the house and started banging his fists on the door, stopping only when the sides of his hands began to smart and he felt himself losing his voice altogether. He gave the door a final, resolute pounding.

This time it opened and he was face to face with Cassie's father. He was holding a hunting rifle, and as David backed away, he pointed it in David's direction and he fired, the shot deliberately missing and kicking up a green, grassy divot just behind David's feet. David smelled gunpowder and, when it dissipated, a whiff of upturned earth.

"The next one," said the doctor, "will kill you."

It was the barrel of the raised weapon, staring at him like a small and unblinking dark eye, that told David it was over, that nothing he could do would change the Germanic blood flowing through his cursed veins, and as he didn't care whether he lived or died at that moment he snarled, "The hell with the both of you," before turning and walking toward the gate.

"Stay away from my daughter!" he heard from behind.

"Go fuck yourself," he yelled into the night air.

When he heard the door of the manor close he began to run, at first slowly and then at full speed, as though fleeing from something impossible to outrun, and as he ran he took huge piercing, bracing draughts of cold night air that left his lungs feeling charred and expanded and alive. He was seventeen and fit, and he ran and he ran and he ran, and when he could finally do so no longer he stopped and put his hands on his knees and coughed up something viscous and pink. He straightened and, still panting, looked around at tall black-brick buildings and empty streets blowing with paper. He was downtown and alone, and he realized at that moment that he had nothing concrete in his life, for he had lost Cassie and his family was disgraced and Mackinnon had fired him from his job at the paper. And because there was nothing left in his young life, he looked up at the constellations and he laughed until his throat hurt and his cheeks ran damp with tears, and he decided to head for Chinatown.

He walked.

When he finally reached The Red Letter, it was the middle of the night and the door was locked, so he had to use the special knock that every young man in the city learned as a rite of passage—two taps, rest, one tap, rest, three taps. The door craned outward and a hulking Cuban Chinese with narrow eyes and earrings opened the door and said with a wink, "Speak easy, my brother," before standing aside.

The place was half-filled with drunks and police and card-playing Asians. David went to the bar and struggled to get the attention of the barkeep. When he finally did, he ordered a whisky. After downing the first one he ordered another. A fog-lit warmth was just enveloping his brain and his body when he heard someone speak directly behind him.

"Hey you."

He turned, prepared for trouble, and saw that one-armed friend of that bastard Sergeant Dunne.

"Ain't you that kid decided to tangle with Mikey Dunne?"

"Suppose I am."

"I'm surprised they let you in."

"What's your name again?"

"Royster."

"David."

"Mind if I call you kid? I ain't so good with names."

"Fine by me."

Royster smiled and in his mouth was a tooth encased in worn tin. "I reckon anyone takes a poke at Mikey Dunne must have some real problems so why don't you let me buy you a drink."

"How's about I buy you one?"

"I'll get the first," said Royster, and it seemed all he had to do was gesture slightly with his remaining arm and the bartender came over immediately and asked what it'd be. "One for me and one for the kid," and so more whisky came and they both drank and to wash away the burn they drank soapy

Prohibition beer that was murky and the colour of a sandy dog's coat. It wasn't long before David was slumped over the bar and telling Royster all about Cassie and all that she'd meant to him and how she'd never even let him fuck her.

"You love her," said Royster.

"I do."

"I can tell you fuckin' do."

"I know I fuckin' do too."

"Listen, kid. Love's a two-headed monster with fangs and a temper."

"Wish I'd known it earlier."

"Well," said Royster. "Only one thing for it."

Royster gestured and Johnny the barkeep came over and Royster ordered two more shots, which they both drank down in a single incinerating gulp. "Let's go," said Royster.

"What do you mean?"

"Like I said. Only one thing for it."

Royster walked away and David felt compelled to follow him. A minute later they were outside, where the cool air made the alcohol explode like a depth-charge in David's veins and muscles and thoughts, and when Royster walked off David noticed it took all of his concentration to walk in a straight line.

"This way, kid," Royster said while looking

over his shoulder. He turned off the main avenue into an alley sided by tenements, and there was a moment in which David feared that perhaps this one-armed man named Royster was setting him up to be robbed. He rid this thought with a shake of head, for the truth of the matter was that, given the way he was feeling, he didn't much care.

"Fuckin' hell," said Royster. "It's like a maze in here, I always get lost …"

They stopped at an intersection of alleyways littered with rotting vegetables. It was dark and he could smell cabbage and he could hear the muffled sound of Chinese being spoken somewhere nearby. There were lamps still burning in some of the windows and this provided the only light in the alleys.

Royster was looking for something, his stump flopping as he turned from one direction to the next.

"I know it's around here somewheres," he said.

"What is?"

"This way," said Royster, and he trundled down one of the alleys and made another turn into yet another alley, this one so narrow it was practically a crevice. There were metal doorways all along, and each was covered with graffiti in both Chinese and English. Royster counted the doors as he walked along, and when he reached the third one on the right he turned and beamed, saying, "Finally. Thought I'd never find the place."

Royster knocked. There came a muffled voice and then the door creaked open, and they were allowed passage by a gap-toothed Caucasian woman with a jet-black wig and a lit cigar. She wore a tight-fitting red silk dress embroidered with dragons and mountain peaks. As David entered, he felt pretty sure that something very bad, or very different, or perhaps some combination of the two, was going to happen to him.

They were in a small cement room lit by an oil lamp with a red glass chimney, which made everything in the room—the sofas, the coffee table, the battered old rug—light up burgundy. The ceiling was so low David could feel his hair touching, and he knew it would come away dusty.

"So," said the woman in a voice deeper than David's. "Look what the cat dragged in."

"Rose," said Royster.

"How are ya, one-arm?"

"Can't complain."

"You brought a friend."

"He's broken-hearted."

"Not for much longer. And yourself?"

"I got something to do in the morning."

"So you won't be staying?"

"I won't."

"We've missed you. Sure I can't tempt you? *Ruby*'s working."

"Can't. I'm dog tired as it is. Any chance I could buy one of those stogies, though?"

Next to one of the sofas was a small end table with a drawer. Rose went to it and pulled out a cigar and, upon handing it to Royster, said, "It's on the house. For the referral."

"Thanks, Rose."

"Next one'll cost you."

"Only fair."

Royster put the cigar in his mouth and lit it with a quick sweep of a metal-case lighter. He grinned and left, and David could hear him singing sad prairie folksongs as he walked down the alley. The woman turned to face David. His heart thrummed with excitement; he was in danger in this place and he knew it and that's why he liked it.

"So," the woman croaked. "Cowboy. Whatta you like?"

"I dunno."

"Whatta ya mean, you dunno? Chink or white. It's a simple question, cowboy."

David swallowed. "White."

"Have a seat. One'll be out in a minute."

There were battered old sofas stretched along two of the room's walls. David sat and as he did he noticed a scent that he preferred not to think about rising from the cushions. For a moment, he wondered whether he wanted to leave. Beaded curtains hung in the doorway, separating the main room from a hallway that led to the rest of the brothel. The curtains parted, and a woman old enough to be David's aunt walked into the room. She was smoking a cigarette and wearing a white wig, and she wore a tight dress with a neckline that plunged to the bottom of her rib cage. David looked at her and for a moment wanted to run, but then his eyes became fixated by the exposed lengths of curvy, paper-white flesh, and it occurred to him that, after the humiliation he'd already endured that evening, a tad more degradation surely wouldn't hurt.

"Hey there, partner."

Her voice was smoky and rough; David marvelled at the way this both repelled and enticed him.

"Hello."

"What's your name?"

"David."

"I'm Brandy. Unless you got another name in mind."

A moment passed between them, during which Brandy smoked and looked bored until finally she said, "Jesus, partner. You coming in or not?"

David stood and followed her through the

beaded doorway. They walked down a barely lit hallway, and when Brandy opened the door to one of the rooms lining the walkway he followed her inside. There was a bed and a low dresser and on the dresser was a basin of water. Other than that, the tiny room was empty. David immediately felt claustrophobic. He also understood that the very thing compelling him to stay was the same thing that made him fearful and want to leave. It was a wonderful contradiction and it consumed all of his attention, and if someone had asked him, at that moment, who "Cassie" was, he would have had to think long and hard.

The woman undressed. She was pale and buxom and did not seem to care in the least that her flesh sagged in places, or that in other places there were faded bruises and small, whorl-shaped puckers or, on the outside of her leg, midway between her knee and her hip, a tattoo of a heart broken in two.

"Whatcha waiting for?"

David undressed. She washed him with warm water and soap that smelled like a mysterious sauce. She hummed as she worked. By the time she deemed him completely clean, he was fully ready and was attempting to kiss her and tell her she was beautiful (for in that moment and in his frame of mind she really, really was).

"Not like that," she said with a throaty laugh. She then led him to the bed and told him to lie down, and then she engulfed him in her smoky, lived-forever essence, and if there was a passage of time it was lost to the gravity of this experience, in this hot and little room, in this seamy and dank and stray dog–infested part of the city. She let him hold her for a minute, and in that minute he felt that he might love this strange woman. But then she rose and he gave his head a shake, and as he pulled on his dungarees he began to chuckle.

This caused her to lighten and ask, "What is it, partner?"

"It's all so ridiculous," he answered.

"What is?"

"The things people do."

"You got that right," she said, and then she laughed and accepted his money and told him that if he was ever broken-hearted again he should just look up ol' Brandy 'cause next time she'd show him some other tricks he wouldn't forget anytime soon.

"Won't be a next time," he said.

"Ahh, they all say that."

"No. I'm serious. I'm gonna enlist."

"In that case, you be careful. I hear things ain't going so well over there."

"Okay," he said, and when he went to give her a goodnight kiss on the cheek she leaned away, looked uncomfortable and sad.

"Not there, partner."

OUTSIDE THE AIR WAS CHILLY and the sky a pale rose hue. The city was just starting to come alive. He went to a Chinese-Canadian diner, where he ate eggs and toast at a lunch counter sticky with jam and spilt sugar. As he ate, he began to feel bad again about Cassie and how much he adored her.

He left feeling exhausted and sore, and for a moment he thought about returning to his graffiti-smeared house. Instead he took a trolley ride downtown, where he walked around as he waited for the 10th Battalion Recruitment Office to open.

When the doors finally opened, he entered and was relieved to see that that prick Sergeant Dunne wasn't there. Instead, he saw a skinny, blond-haired officer. His name tag read *Carmichael*.

"Good day," he said.

David sat, and he watched the man sift through

some papers on his desk. He looked up and, with widened eyes, asked, "It's Mann, isn't it?"

"Yeah, you got it. How did you know?"

"I can't enlist you."

Though David expected this reply, he still feigned surprise. "Why not?"

"I don't know. I have a list here with ineligibles and you're on it. Fact is, you're right at the top."

"That's bullshit."

"It may be, but I got my orders. And I'll thank you not to use that kind of language in this office."

"Sorry."

"Have you been convicted of any crimes lately?"

"Of course not."

"And you have no physical infirmities?"

"None that I know of."

"You a pervert?"

"Should I be?"

"That I don't know."

"I'd like to speak to your boss."

"How do you know I have one?"

David didn't answer. The officer rolled his eyes slightly and said, "All right."

He rose and walked away toward an office in the corner, and when he returned he did nothing but motion with a finger. David followed him. In the office was a tubby major with a handlebar moustache. When he spoke with an English accent, David was not at all surprised.

"Sit," said the major.

David did so.

"So, your wish is to join the army."

"It is."

The major chuckled cruelly. "And we *are* talking about the Canadian Army?"

David understood everything.

"Listen to what I'm telling you, son. You'd have a better chance of flying to the moon than being enlisted in any office I run."

"That so."

"The apple, as they say, never falls far from the tree. We've already relieved your sister of her duties."

David narrowed his eyes and then reached into the pocket of his jacket, where he still had about two months' worth of wages. As the major watched, he carefully straightened the money and placed it halfway across the major's dcsk. It sat there for the longest time. The major stared at a spot on the desktop that was halfway between the money and the young man who had produced it. His stubby fingertips met beneath his nose, and he swivelled from side to side in his leather chair.

Finally, his eyes looked up and met David's. He leaned forward.

"I'll be frank, you galling little shit. There's a war on and there's a very real possibility we're going to run out of men to fight it."

He took the money in fat pink fingers turned orange at the tips.

"So we do what we have to do. That's always been my motto. There's a train leaving in two days."

"I'll be on it."

"I'm sure you will."

David said nothing and left, choosing to walk all the way to his graffiti-coated house; his legs ached and he thought for hours and hours and he realized that there was nothing, not one thing, that felt right in his life. When he arrived home, he saw something sitting on the doorstep. It was a small box. He bent over and picked it up and opened it.

It was the St. George medal that Cassie wore on a thin silver chain around her neck. As he looked at it, he couldn't help but picture the place where it rested on her young, white chest. His heart pounded.

There was a small note, folded beside the necklace.

Dearest David,

When you came to my window I wanted nothing more than to come down and see you and hold you and kiss you, but you know my father would have killed me. Please believe me when I say I don't care what your father may or may not have done ... please! I've done nothing but think of you, and all the times we had together, and now I hear that you're going off to war! David I can't bear it—I really can't. Please accept this as a keepsake of my love for you. Please take it with you and keep it with you at all times.

Oh David, please come home safe!

With love, Cassie

He read it again and again and again. He looked up at the sky, which was blue and distant and scattered with thin streaky clouds. It occurred to him that one day, he might understand such things as war and ambition and the demons that take hold of men, but he knew that the one thing he would never understand, no matter how long he lived, was the life-force that breathed in the heart of a woman.

TEN

O N THE FIRST MORNING in which she felt
close to normal, Sarah left Dunne's room
and went shopping. It was not hard to avoid
places where she normally shopped, not in this
neighbourhood of egg stores and noodle stands.
She bought bread, Chinese wine, cooked chicken
legs, whatever fresh fruit she could find and a brick
of rationed cheese that was hard and white and
smelled like wax. She then went to Eaton's, where
a saleswoman wearing thin white cotton gloves
helped her buy a blue gingham dress with straps

that went over her shoulders. Sarah hoped that her sergeant would like it.

She returned to the room and found him laying dressed on top of the made bed. He was reading a newspaper while smoking. He looked up and moved to help her with her purchases.

"No more diner food for you," she said. "It's bad for the stomach."

Together, they moved the small table in the room next to the window, which Sarah opened to let in the cool, early afternoon breeze.

"There's only one chair," she said.

"I'll go."

Dunne smiled weakly and left. From inside the room, she could hear him knocking, first on one door and then another. Meanwhile, she slipped out to the bathroom and put on her new dress. She then looked at herself in the mirror, gauging her hair and her skin in a way that felt strange to her. When she heard him return, she pinched both of her cheeks and felt like a foolish schoolgirl.

She went back to the room. He had his back to her and was placing another chair at the table.

"There's an old pensioner down the hall," he said. "His door was open. I'll put it back when we're done. He won't even notice it."

Dunne turned and, in his eyes, Sarah saw the

same fraught awakening that she herself was experiencing. "Do you like it?"

"Sarah, you look …"

She waited for him to locate the right word, and when he was unable she went to him and kissed him on the mouth for the first time and said only, "Let's eat."

For the next hour or so they sat at the window, eating cheese and bread and apples and watching the bustle on the street below them; as they ate, they imagined that the busy people outside were looking up and seeing them and feeling jealous of the couple in the window. The chicken was overcooked and stringy and they didn't care. The wine, too, was poor, but after several juice glasses' worth, its taste began to take on an astringent familiarity, as though it were something they'd known for all of their lives and that made them feel whole again. Soon they felt warm and content and embraced by the feeling that *that* afternoon had been delivered for one reason only, and that was to please them.

When they were both full and there was no more wine, they smoked cigarettes and looked at each other through hazy blue spirals. When these were finished, they wordlessly stood and held each other in arms turned weak and weightless.

"Sarah …"

"Shhh."

She led him to the bed, where they each took turns slowly undressing the other, with a tenderness often reserved for children. When they lay down next to each other, all Sarah had to do was close her eyes and kiss the salty recess between his shoulder and neck. She and the sergeant both melted into nothingness, only to emerge as a single writhing warm form, oblivious of time and place and the sad, strange events that make people the way they are.

When they finally returned to the confines of their bodies, the sun had long ago left their window, and the light in the room was burnished and low. Dunne took two cigarettes and gave one to Sarah. He lit hers before his own. They smoked, saying nothing, and then Sarah turned and traced her fingertips over his upper body, which was marred with scars and dents and past trauma. Her voice was whispery and calm.

"Where did you get this?"

"Kitcheners Wood. April 22nd, 1915."

"And this one?"

She watched as he tried to glimpse the top of his own chest. "*That*? That was from a rodeo in North Battlefield. I had the pleasure of drawing a bronco who took a natural dislike to me."

"And this?"

Dunne paused. "Was a bullet went through there."

"Where?"

"Vimy."

"Your body's like a map."

"If so, it's a map leading nowhere."

She lay her head on his chest and felt a peacefulness she'd not known for a considerable time. She could hear his heartbeat and the tranquil, repetitive hush of his breathing. He lit another cigarette and for a moment the room filled with a whiff of sulphur and smoking wood. Were it possible, she thought, she might have lain this way forever.

"Sarah," he finally said. "Don't go back to that house for a while."

"My brother's there."

"He's a grown man."

"He's also one that needs taking care of. He's a dreamer, Michael Dunne. Never an ounce of sense. Head in the stars. He's always needed taking care of. Always."

"Still. I'm just saying."

Sarah Mann stayed. Dunne did not report for duty until the day came when Major Dobson-Hughes accused him, via a delivered note, of insubordination. He also wrote that Dunne could expect an official reprimand leading to reassignment.

Sarah was there when he read it; it was the first time, she noticed, that she saw her sergeant smile fully, as though merriment belonged on his heavily lined features.

They slept late in the mornings. After groggily waking, they'd go out for coffee and maybe toast. Then they'd go to the market, where they'd pick out ingredients for that day's lunch—a variation on that first day's, though sometimes they'd get ham slices instead of chicken, or bottles of a local, malty lager instead of rice wine. They had picnics in a nearby park, amid schoolchildren and young widows and those who spent their days sleeping on benches. Here they ate and drank and then lay looking at clouds. They also talked, her sergeant full of stories whenever the conversation steered toward his life before the war—it seemed that he'd done pretty much everything, at least once, and whether it was a legal pursuit or not never seemed to have had much bearing on his decision to do it. She also noticed that whenever the conversation drifted toward wartime, her sergeant would grow quiet and grave, as if there were something colouring his impression of the world over there. At times, she swore she could *see* that something, eating at his thoughts, swallowing his ability to be happy, and she had to force herself not to ask him what it was.

After lunch, they ended up in the same place: in Michael Dunne's squeaking bed, exploring each other with fingertips and mouths and hair lightened by the sun streaming brown through the room's grimy window, until they both reached a place where problems and wartime no longer existed. They smoked cigarettes and laughed about nothing and when they rose to go out for dinner it was preceded by a long walk through town. After a light dinner—lunch had become their major meal of the day—they'd return to Dunne's rooming house and let their passions arise under the cloak of darkness. Once, they went to the movies in an "atmospheric" movie house that had stars painted on the ceiling and camels on the walls and pillars framing the screen that had been moulded to look like palm trees, all in the effort to make the cinema look like an Arabian desert. The film they saw was *Intolerance* by D.W. Griffith, and though Sarah was not overly moved by it—she was too conscious of the nearness of her sergeant's forearm, and the scent emanating from his jacket—she noticed that Dunne said little afterwards, and then woke several times that night, gasping and clawing at the sheets and thinking that he was back in Europe. His chest pitched and heaved and he was covered in a light film of perspiration.

"Shhh, Michael. It's a dream."

"No," he said. "It ain't."

"Shhh," she said again. "I'm here."

Finally, she got him to lie back down and breathe deeply and when he finally calmed himself he confessed to her.

"Thing is," he said, "when I have these dreams, they seem realer than anything. They seem realer than this city, than the streets outside our window. They seem realer than you and me, lying here."

"You're shell-shocked."

"Most are," he said.

"And most probably feel the same way you do."

He rotated his head on the pillow and looked at her; for a single moment, she was sure she saw a slight issuance of comfort in his eyes. She fell back asleep holding him, though when she awoke he was still gazing up at the ceiling.

DUNNE BOUGHT HER SMALL ITEMS to keep her going—toothpaste, a hairbrush, items of apparel that she selected at Woolworth's while he stood outside smoking. Yet neither of them was rich and she had never packed a bag and finally, on their fourth day together, she could stand it no longer.

"I have to go home and get some things."

He looked at her and was about to protest when he realized she was right.

"I'll go with you."

It was midmorning. They shared a trolley with servicemen and housewives, and were dropped off a few blocks from Sarah's house. To Sarah's relief, there were no louts standing around outside, though the house had gathered more blood-red graffiti and she noticed that one of the windows around the side of the house was broken.

"Look at it," she said.

"Nothing a bit of paint and a good handyman couldn't fix. This will all blow over, Sarah."

"I hope you're right."

They stood there for the longest time before she pointed to some movement in the window. "David's home," she said. "I need to talk to him."

"You want me to wait outside?"

She thought. "No, it's fine. He and I need to have a long talk. I'll meet you back at the room."

"You sure?"

She nodded and felt awkward kissing him in front of the other weather-beaten houses in the neighbourhood—it was as though these poor homes had eyes, trained on her and everything she did.

Dunne squeezed her hand and turned to leave. She went up the front walk, pushed open the door and saw David at the kitchen table, arranging the contents of a suitcase he'd acquired from his father. It took her a few seconds to understand what this all meant—David, a suitcase, the war—though when she did it was with the realization that sometimes the most obvious facts are the hardest to perceive. She sighed and felt tired all over.

She sat at the table and watched him.

"When?"

"When what?"

"When do you go?"

"Couple of hours."

"Oh, David."

"Don't."

"You're a *boy*."

He closed the suitcase and glared at her. "Not any more."

"You're too young."

"What's done is done."

She was on the verge of tears. "Oh God, they can't let you …"

"Sister," he said, "they didn't have a problem at all. Listen, I've gotta go."

He stood and headed toward the door, though before he could leave she called out: "Please, David, please. Talk to Sergeant Dunne. He'll tell you not to go."

She grabbed at his arms, and when David spun around there was hatred in his eyes. It was only because she knew him that she understood it was not meant specifically for her. "He could explain to them and they would let you out …"

"What makes you think they'd listen to him? Jesus, Sarah. You think he's some kind of hero? Is he missing an arm or a leg? Is he blind? So then why isn't he over there?"

"David!"

"He's shell-shocked, Sarah. He's a coward."

She slapped him and felt the burn on her hand spread to the whole of her slight, pale body.

Alone in the house, it felt empty and frightening and cold; she sat shivering at the kitchen table, wishing for tablets and the speckled, shimmering relief they brought her. Through dampened eyes, she looked at all the things in this room, and at that moment it seemed to her that every object— every cupboard, every utensil, every slat in the chipped, pale-green floorboard—delivered to her memories she wished she didn't have.

I hate it here, she thought.

She stayed at the table for the longest time, for she hoped that the feelings she had at that moment would seep into the marrow of her bones, forcing her to carry out her rough plans—she would leave this place, maybe she could sell the land underneath it, and she would use her savings to get away once and for all, and she hoped that Dunne would go with her.

Sarah sat and she brooded and this was good, for it caused her resolve to grow stronger. She packed her own suitcase with clothes, and when leaving wondered how many more times she'd step inside this place. Before going to Sergeant Dunne's room, she walked to the Queen's Park cemetery. Here, she swept the leaves and gravel from her mother's gravesite. Lowering herself, she stared at the cool granite marker—it was a small cross chiselled with roses—and then she told her mother that David was going off to war and she had fallen in love with a soldier named Dunne who had trouble with authority and that everyone knew about Daddy now, and because of this they'd painted the house and called ugly things to her, and that she'd had trouble with some medicine at the hospital, but she was fine now and *How could Daddy have done that? How could he have chosen that side? Didn't he think how that would affect us?* and she told her mother that there still wasn't a day in which she didn't think of the times when she was little and they would bake together or go for walks in the park and *Oh, oh, Ma, when will the crevice you left inside me finally heal over?*

Above her, there were songbirds and bright sun and spools of thin, drifting cloud. The voice that spoke came from inside her head.

My darling, she heard. *There is more virtue in patience than charity or honour or faith.*

There is?

Yes, my darling. There is.

Sarah leaned forward and let her lips touch cool granite; she tasted dirt and cement dust and a fine residue of quartz. She rose and straightened her skirt and walked to Dunne's rooming house, letting herself in with the key he'd copied for her. He wasn't in. She waited next to the window, and she occupied herself by mending some of the clothes she'd brought with her. She hummed as she worked, a tune her mother had sung softly whenever she'd felt reflective or distant or unloved.

When Michael Dunne returned, Sarah met him with a forced smile. Over the next half-hour, it became more and more difficult to feign cheer—she could feel her own fatigue drape over her like a veil.

"Sarah," her sergeant finally said. "What's the matter?"

"Nothing," she said. "Nothing at all."

She then put her face in her small, trembling hands and allowed herself to weep.

ELEVEN

WHEN SHE FINALLY SPOKE, her voice was a strangled croak. "He'll get himself killed over there. I know it. I know it. He needs someone to look after him. He's the only family I have in this world. He's trying to prove something that's pointless and I can't stop him."

Dunne looked at her and felt strange. For the first time since he'd returned from the war, the unreality radiating from all objects evaporated, leaving things clean and pure and the way they really were. The guilt that hounded him at all times—for killing that boy, for having the temerity to fall in love, for being the person that he was—subsided and then disappeared altogether.

"What do I do?" he asked.

"Hold me," she said, and they made love in the manner of those who can think of no other way to divert attention from their own searing misfortune. Sarah sniffled throughout, though when he moved to stop, thinking he was hurting her somehow, she held him tighter to her and said, "Don't you dare."

He put her to bed and in a moment she was asleep, her breathing a noiseless rise and fall. For the next several hours, he lay awake, listening to the noises coming from the other rooms: arguments and snoring and grinding bedsprings and sad, off-key singing. With time, these sounds died down as well, and the only thing Dunne could hear was Sarah's occasional rustling and the chatter of his own nervous thoughts. He rose, dressed and left the room, knowing full well that he would not be returning anytime soon. He felt a remorse that was delicious and intense.

It was dark, and the first of the fallen leaves made skittering insect sounds when they blew over the streets of Chinatown. He walked and walked, invested with a sureness he had not known often in life, and when he reached the bungalow belonging to Major Dobson-Hughes he felt pleased. He looked around. The yards were all well kept and pretty in this neighbourhood. Though many of them held a scattering of children's toys, he knew from scouring the files in the recruitment office that the major lived alone.

He took a breath and walked around back. He was carrying the dagger he'd been issued at Vimy, and when he reached the back door he used its tip to try to spring the lock embedded in the door's handle. He jiggled and jiggled and cursed himself for not being better at this. After a time he gave up and looked around the major's yard for something he could use. He saw nothing until he went around the side of the small clapboard house and found a few half-empty paint cans. Next to the cans was a rag splattered in paint; he took it and wrapped it around his right hand, then he chanced waking the major by punching out the glass in the rear door of the house.

There was a clatter of broken glass on linoleum. Dunne stopped and listened, and heard nothing beyond a high, happy whine in his ears. He reached in and unlocked the door from the inside and walked over shards of spent glass.

He could hear the major snoring and it was a sound he found repulsive. He followed it toward the major's room and walked in through the half-opened door. He pulled a high-back chair next to the bed and sat and watched the major, thinking, I could kill you in a second. In a half-second.

Dunne cleared his throat, expecting this would wake the major. Dunne cleared his throat a second time, and when this didn't work he said, "Wake up, for chrissakes," and when this failed too he reached out and shook the major by the shoulder. The older man came awake, sputtering. His eyes widened with fear, though only briefly; as soon as he was fully awake, his eyes narrowed, his expression now one of venom. Dunne had his knife out again, and he noticed that the major kept taking quick, flitting glances at it.

"How the hell did you get in here?"

Dunne didn't answer. Dobson-Hughes moved to get out of bed, and when he did Dunne pushed him back down hard.

"You can take any one of them. Artillery, gas, rats, rain, bayonet—not one of these you can control. Matches you control. You can have some effect on them. And when you're in the middle of a barrage and you think a smoke might steady you up and you reach for those matches and they're wet? Well, your whole world feels like it's buckling, like it's coming apart at the seams, and that's not farce, you bloated old windbag. That's not farce."

"What the hell are you doing here?"

"Got somethin' I need from you."

"How'd you get in?"

"Broke a window."

"I could have you arrested."

"If they ever let me out, I'd kill you."

The major paused. "You're a coward," he hissed.

"Must be. I killed a child over there."

"It happens."

"It didn't have to."

"It's bloody well the sort of thing that *does* happen, doesn't it? In South Africa, I saw them speared with bayonets."

"Who?"

"Babies, sergeant. Little black Zulu babies. It made your eyes film over and your soul die and your heart blacken. You think it affected my duty?"

"Maybe it should've."

"Well it didn't, sergeant. It bloody well *didn't*. We weren't allowed, is the short of it. You think we even *had* shell shock back then? Christ, no, it was *Clean up this mess chaps and if I see any blubbering you'll be in the brigade until you grow a pair of bollocks, now get on with it*, and the next day there was another village and more women and children and horrors to be visited."

"It shouldn't've been that way."

"Most things *shouldn't*."

"You were supposed to be the civilized ones."

"Civility, sergeant, has nothing to do with it. If you're not willing to fight fire with fire, then you'll lose."

Dunne paused and looked at the major and felt a sparking of rage. He considered busting the major hard in the jaw with the handle of his knife. Instead he reached into his jacket pocket and pulled out a sheet of paper.

"Sign this," said Dunne.

"What is it?"

"An enlistment form."

The major picked it up and read it and looked back puzzled at the sergeant. "Who on earth is MacCrae?"

"I am. It's my mother's maiden name."

"You want to go *back*?"

"Always did. Sign it or I'll kill you."

"I imagine you would. I do know, by the way, about your past. No stranger to the inside of a jail cell, are we?"

"Sign the fucking thing."

Dobson-Hughes smirked while he signed. Again, Dunne had the desire to hit him.

"It was a pleasure doing business with you," said Dobson-Hughes. "Things over there are *not* going swimmingly. I dare say you'll have a fine time."

"Fuck you," said Michael Dunne.

Dunne rose and left the way he came in. As he stepped into the cool windswept night he heard the old major chuckle and say, "Don't forget to close the door behind you, old man. You wouldn't want me to catch my death …"

DUNNE REACHED THE EDGE OF TOWN just as the skies were beginning to turn violet. He put out his thumb on a road leading into the mountains and waited for ages. Finally, a grizzled logger in an empty transport vehicle stopped and, over the chug of his engine, called out, "You need a lift, soldier?"

"I do," said Dunne as he climbed aboard.

"Name's Wilson."

"MacCrae."

"Where you headed?"

"Up a ways."

"Only thing up a ways is mountains."

"Not quite the only thing. By the way, how'd you know I was a soldier?"

"Just did."

For the rest of the way the two men fell into a silence that Dunne did not find uncomfortable. After forty-five minutes he said, "Here," and when the logger pulled over they were next to a slight, grassy impression that led in the direction of Brant Lake.

"You got a hunting cabin up there, son?"

"Something like that."

Dunne had a backpack and in it was food and liquor.

"You sure you wanna be dropped off *here*?"

"Like I said. Much obliged."

Dunne set off toward the homestead, and when he reached it the morning had arrived sunny and glorious. He spent the day bothered by memory and thoughts of Sarah. Around noon he took a walk through some pine woods and was not careful about keeping his bearings; he emerged in a clearing with the homestead in sight and wondered how he'd managed to come full circle. Then he started drinking, slowly but surely, thinking it'd be a long time before he saw another bottle of rye whisky. By the end of the afternoon, he was maudlin and stumbling and worried that all of the things he'd done in his life lacked meaning or purpose. It then occurred to him that maybe *all* things—not just things involving his own directionless life—lacked reason or purpose or meaning of any kind. For some reason this thought cheered him a little.

He went out to the grave marker he had carved and saw no reason to change it. From here he watched the sun set behind the mountains, turning the opposite valley a hundred shades of orange and then red. When the sun had set he stumbled back to the cabin and by the light of an oil lamp with a cracked glass chimney he sat with a pen and paper.

He started writing several times, and each time he stopped and crumpled up the paper and then cursed his own sad inability with words. Frustrated, he took a break to eat something, and when he returned to the task he still felt awkward and weak.

Dearest Sarah, he wrote. *I'm not sure if you'll get this and I don't know if I'm so good at painting pictures in my head, but I'm trying. In this picture, there is a river and there is a horse and there is a man sitting on that horse and together they ford that river and all these things are in the foothills.*

He paused and felt better.

When this man closes his eyes, he can conjure up a fire. And he can see a woman sitting next to him on a bed that's never been slept in. And he can feel her kissing him as like as to smother him. And this man knows that kings may die and countries may crumble but people will keep going. And if we look close enough, we just might, as I have, Sarah, we just might find something to believe in. I have to go now, but before I do I promise you I remember the rule you gave me, the one where you

said I couldn't die and that's a rule I accept, Sarah,
as a condition of my going. That's one rule, Sarah,
I won't kick against screaming.

Dunne reread the letter several times and each time he thought it poor. When he finally slept, it was at the rickety little desk where he was sitting, his face supported by his forearms. The oil lamp burned until it ran out of fuel and the soot caking the chimney started to smoke. He awoke the next morning with a thirst and a powerful head. He stayed for another two days. On his fourth morning, he tromped through dew-soaked grass back down to the roadway and waited for a ride. Upon reaching the city, he put Sarah's note in the mail, and he then boarded a train heading east to Toronto, where they sent him for ten bullshit days of basic training at a military defence base near a town called Orillia—at this juncture in the war, with soldiers so desperately needed in Europe, recruits were shown how to load and shoot a rifle, how to bayonet a straw-filled Kraut, how to march around the perimeters of a cornfield, how to keep their feet dry in the trenches, how to avoid contracting syphilis in European bordellos (*Make sure it's one hundred per cent goatskin, fellows*) and not much else.

From here, Dunne departed for Montreal and the send-off town of Sydney, Nova Scotia.

PASSCHENDAELE

ONE

HE SAILED ON THE S.S. *BLYTHEWOOD*, a thirty-seven-year-old private in a hold full of farmboys and miners' sons and skinny high-school dropouts—they had a habit of not seeing him and, if they did, they referred to him as *sir*. He did not tell anyone that he'd made this same trip two years earlier, or that he'd been at Vimy, or that he'd been promoted to sergeant, or that he'd won a medal, or that he'd come within a hair's breadth of being shot for desertion. He responded to the name *MacCrae* and, occasionally, *mister*.

They were kept below in large dormitory quarters that should have held a third of their numbers. The bunks, which were stacked three high and placed in four rows running the length of the ship, were bolted to the floor, so as to prevent them from toppling during one of the storms that, Dunne knew, would likely assault the ship during its passage. They were fed gummy stews flavoured with curry to mask the gamey flavour of the beef. They pissed in trough urinals and they showered in a single cramped, mouldy-tiled room. When they were let up for air, the officers warned them not to fall overboard, for if the temperature of the water didn't kill them, drowning or panic or sharks most certainly would.

At first, the other recruits forced themselves to be celebratory. As they waited in the protection of Sydney Harbour—it took almost two days to load the ship with all of the necessary supplies—they sang war songs and played cards and had the occasional punch-up following accusations of cheating. Dunne, whose bunk was in the corner of the hold, kept to himself, reading and thinking of Sarah and, most of all, banking his sleep. He quickly figured out that David Mann was not on board, which did not surprise Dunne or worry him excessively.

There were other older recruits, and Dunne

could tell they were running away from something: they all had an excess of lines on the face, their eyes never rested, and they smoked continually, from the moment they awoke to the moment they fell asleep. There were times when Dunne would wake in the middle of the night and see the tell-tale glow of cigarettes moving up and down in the darkness, and hear the sound of smoky breath being exhaled.

Mostly, they kept to themselves.

THE SHIP LEFT HARBOUR on a Tuesday. It was so foggy and damp that the soldiers' wool uniforms became wet, and when they came down below the moisture from the uniforms turned into a damp cloud that settled on the inside of the hold; soon the walls ran with droplets. Dunne remembered this happening on his first trip over, and he knew that as the ship gathered steam, the heat from the engine would pump into the servicemen's quarters, turning the atmosphere stifling and claustrophobic. The farmhands and east-coasters—men used to filling their lungs with fresh air—were the first turned quiet and taciturn by the conditions. Soon, others followed suit. The room filled with the foul, septic odour of young men who were sweating and had no way to keep their clothing or bedding clean. Portholes were kept closed against the cold. Many joked that the bunks were so narrow that if you wanted to roll onto your other side, you had to get out of bed to do so—by the second or third day of the voyage, the joke failed to elicit chortles and instead was spoken as a grim complaint.

The food, too, became oppressive. While the young men had, at first, been impressed by its quantity—*quite fillin', this* was a common refrain—the heavy curry taste began to bother them, as did the absence of fruit or fresh bread or milk that did not suffer from a slightly curdled quality. Furthermore, it was a chore to eat; the sea rolled so heavily that the stew had a tendency to slop out of the bowl, such that by the time mess was over there was food spilled everywhere, most noticeably on the laps and sleeves of the recruits. The lack of oxygen caused headaches and snoring, and the continual grind of the piston engine began to wear on the nerves of the younger soldiers. Many now spent their time in the same way as Dunne: lying on their backs, attempting to sleep their way through the passage. When awake, they would stare at photographs given to them by their sweethearts (many of whom had presented their soldier-boys with pictures that verged on the risqué—an exposed shoulder, the top buttons of a blouse left undone, a whiff of suggestion in their glance. And while many of the recruits had been delighted by this at first, they now resented it, for it served only to increase their longing for home and things representing comfort).

On the fourth day, a storm hit, and even those who had shown no sign of seasickness became ill; the odour of vomit now added to the melange of smells in the soldiers' hold. Desperate, men went up on deck to be sick, though they were so afraid of falling into the ocean they clung to the centre of the deck. Here, they spewed on their hands and knees, rain pelting against their backs, only to clean it up themselves or risk the wrath of the officers (who all carried pistols as a general means of dissuading mutinous fervour, of which there was plenty). Men stopped reporting for mess, though it soon came down that the officers interpreted this as insubordination; the men then had to enact an absurd ritual in which they sat at the long, plank-like mess tables, their complexions as green as the skin of a frog, holding the sides of their bowls as their uneaten rations slopped onto the table. At night, Dunne heard whimpers and prayer. He, too, felt nauseated and weak, and he began to suffer from fantasies involving self-harm.

On the ninth day, word went round: *Land ho!* Everyone rushed on board and risked falling into the churning seas, and when they were ordered back down below, they were all happy and relieved and once again they behaved like jubilant boys. This lasted for no longer than an hour; Plymouth Harbour was so crowded with munitions ships, troop carriers and tramp steamers that they had to wait outside the shelter of the harbour, where the rough waters continued to rock the ship from side to side. This frustration—they were so *close*—was the final straw, and the slightest gesture resulted in fisticuffs. Fights broke out over perceived slights, over suspect card deals, over glances taken the wrong way; from the cocoon of his bunk, Dunne watched his fellow sailors decorate themselves with bruises and lacerations and eyes ringed with purple-black. Yet the moment the ship's engines throttled back up, and the ship began moving into a lane that would take it through the rocky entrance to the harbour, the fighting stopped, as if by command. In fact, those young men who had most viciously battered one another emerged from the ship as the closest of friends. The same thing had happened to Dunne on his first crossing—he'd ended up exchanging addresses with a stocky Edmontonian who had, a half-day earlier, attempted to hit Dunne in the face with the base of a milk pitcher. Though the sergeant didn't quite understand this phenomenon, he knew well that it existed, and under what conditions it flourished.

The trains were waiting. The men piled on

board, many of them expressing surprise that there was a seat for everyone; Dunne noticed that their gratitude made them seem young, even if the days had long passed in which their faces were unlined and their expressions wide-eyed. Dunne sat next to a kid from northern British Columbia who looked to have a little Native in him; like the others, he cheered when the train left the station, and he cheered again when porters came around with trays of thick black ale that the young men didn't particularly like but drank anyway.

One of the officers entered the car in which Dunne sat.

"All right lads," he said. "We know it was a rough crossing and this is the chief's way of saying thank you. Have one on us, and when you're done have another!"

A cheer went round, and when the infantrymen had finished their pints they looked around expectantly, as if willing the porters to appear. They were given their second ale and Dunne drank his with a feeling that was close to déjà vu, albeit tinged with regret and longing.

It was around the time they'd finished their second pints—many wore foam moustaches and somehow this made them look all the more innocent—that something odd happened. He'd expected the ale to heighten their relief at being off the ship; he'd even resigned himself to singing popular songs with them, like "Pack Up Your Troubles in Your Old Kit Bag" or "It's a Long Way to Tipperary." He needn't have worried. With their second pints frothing in their stomachs, the men mostly rested back in their seats and looked worried. Dunne felt it too; there was something about this trip through the English countryside that was different from the one he'd taken two years ago, something ominous and draining and present.

With a start, he realized what it was—the country was pitch-black. No matter how hard he looked through the rail-carriage window, he could not pick out a single burning light; it was as though they were pushing through unmanned darkness, even the moon refusing to shine. The train rumbled through the night. Although everyone quieted, few actually slept.

The morning came up weak and pale blue; the weather wasn't rain but something close to it. He missed Sarah, and felt like a fool for leaving her. Other than that, he felt calmer than he had in ages. Midmorning, the train pulled into a station marked *Elham*. As they filed onto the tiny open-air platform, Dunne overheard one of the officers remark that Dover was close enough that a weak man could hit it from here with a stone. They were marched along muddy roads for two hours, and when they stopped it was in front of a large manor that, someone said, had been lent to the army effort by its gentleman owner. They filed in and found each room filled with cots; a sense of jubilation once again flitted through the young men, and they ran around testing beds and arguing over who would sleep in which room. Everyone picked a cot, and when the cots ran out those who still needed a place to sleep set up lean-tos in the backyard of the manor, bragging about being out of doors and away from the stench of unwashed socks.

That afternoon, they were assembled in the manor's great room, where they stripped and were examined by a medic looking, once again, for signs of lice, pox, mumps, skin disease, piles, venereal disease, rickets or consumption. Toes were touched and private parts lifted. The vast majority passed, though it turned out that a few of the recruits were insane, and that another handful were no more than fourteen—how they had snuck through was anybody's guess—and arrangements were made to send these recruits home. The rest were issued their kit and the rest of their uniforms: peaked cap, high-collared khaki jacket, brown boots, woollen puttees, gas mask, collarless grey shirt, thick woollen socks, undergarments, sleeved vest, overcoat and two coarse grey blankets. Each man was also given a rifle with bayonet and told that losing said weapon was a treasonous act and punishable by execution.

They spent two nights in the manor and then they were marched back to the train station and taken to the port at Dover, where they were packed into a series of ferries that transported them over the English Channel. The men were feeling good after two days of proper rest. With the sun shining and the air crisp and each one feeling proud, they really did start singing, for it had occurred to them all that they were about to land in northern France and that *this* was where the war was being fought. In Calais, they boarded a final train and were taken to a small Belgian town called Poperinge; here, they were billeted in an old, crumbling, green-walled hospital for the criminally insane.

The hospital had been jury-rigged to accommodate the soldiers. The inmates, packed twice as many per cell as usual, had been pushed into the northern wing. About three hundred soldiers, all of them waiting to bolster infantry battalions in the front, occupied the southern half of the building. Each soldier was registered, given a pamphlet on the transmission of syphilis and gonorrhea and told to await orders. Most of the men chose to do this outside, where several dozen games of soccer were simultaneously taking place, all under the watch of the madmen, who gazed at the young soldiers through windows protected by wire mesh.

Dunne went outside and let his face warm in the high sun. There were hundreds of soldiers, representing all parts of Canada. It wasn't long before he spotted his old friend, the Sarcee Indian called Highway. Dunne went up and tapped him on the shoulder, and when the Indian turned a look of confusion washed over his face.

"*Mikey?*"

"One and the same."

"I thought they were gonna shoot you."

"They said I was crazy so I was spared that particular experience."

"Man, I don't get it. What the hell are you *doing* here?"

Dunne ignored the question. Instead he asked, "I don't suppose you've run across a kid named David Mann? By the way, my name's MacCrae now. I had to re-enlist under false pretences."

Highway looked at him. "So you really are crazy."

"As a hoot owl, apparently."

"Well. It's good to see that nothin's changed. C'mon."

Dunne followed him back to the group of men with whom Highway had been talking. One by one,

Dunne shook hands with Highway's friends from the 10th, some of whom had torn through London with him before being redeployed. There was a short guy in his early twenties named Cahill; a lanky man in his late twenties named Witchell; a young French Canadian named Godin; a big, burly man named Johnson; another guy named Miles; and an intense, nervous-looking soldier named Horne. Each time Highway introduced Dunne as Mikey MacCrae, he did so with a smirk.

Dunne talked with Highway and his friends for long enough to learn that they'd been stuck at the hospital forever, and that they were all going insane with boredom, and that when it came right down to it, being in the trenches was a better prospect than standing around all day in a loony bin brooding over the thought of *being* in the trenches. Dunne smiled and agreed that waiting was the worst part. After a bit he told Highway that he wanted to explore the grounds a bit more.

"Mikey," said Highway. "Jeez, it's good to see you."

"It's good to see you too, Highway."

The grounds were a huge muddy field surrounded by a low wall topped with bits of broken bottles set into cement. Beyond the fence was a pasture growing with flax and trees. As he walked along the perimeter of the yard, he passed group after group of young men, all talking and smoking cigarettes and making claims of the things they'd do once they finally got out of here—most of the claims, Dunne noticed, had to do with farmgirls and killing Huns. He saw men pass photographs of their sweethearts, and he overheard one man claim he was afraid of nothing but nothing and if Fritz thought he was, well he was damn wrong. At the corner of the yard, where the wall turned back toward the rear of the hospital, Dunne stopped and looked in the direction of the sea—though he couldn't see it he could taste it on his tongue. Above him were kestrels and low-lying clouds and the spectres created by a disturbed memory. He started to walk back toward Highway's bunch.

About halfway along the wall, a young man talking to two others turned to spit the taste of tobacco off his tongue. He then looked up and locked eyes with Dunne; Dunne watched, not surprised, as those eyes flared with resentment.

TWO

T HE TWO MEN AVOIDED EACH OTHER for the next couple of days. This was not difficult. David's bunk was in one of the rooms on the third floor of the hospital, whereas Dunne was sleeping in the hospital's dining room, which had been converted into a large, wood-panelled dormitory. In mess, they kept an eye out, ensuring they occupied positions as far away as possible from each other at the long, papered tables. During recreation, there seemed to be an implicit, unspoken agreement that they keep a constant distance between them, like two planets in orbit around each other.

At night, Dunne lay awake, listening to artillery shells in the distance. In the mornings following an assault, the yard smelled of cordite and churned earth. Off in the distance, he could sometimes see a low-lying, yellow-brown mist, and this was worrisome. He caught himself pining for the obliviousness of the recent enlistees, who continued to play soccer and smoke cigarettes and talk about the imagined wonders of Belgian girls. Several times a day, the intermittent wails coming from the other side of the hospital would coalesce, like something infectious, and soon every inmate from the north wing would be howling and screaming and reaching their arms through the barred windows, as if trying to claw their way out of hell. This would go on for twenty minutes, sometimes even thirty, and it never failed to shatter the nerves of the enlistees in the yard, who shuffled as far away as possible, some even managing to scale the wall without cutting themselves in the process. Then the insane would go quiet, as though some aggregate comment had been fully expressed.

Mostly Dunne kept to himself, though when he did feel like socializing it was with Highway and his friends, who were aware that there was another 10th Battalion member, a young kid bunking on the top floor; for whatever reason, the kid was choosing to keep his distance. This changed on Dunne's fifth day in the hospital. It was a cool afternoon in mid-October, and he was leaning against the wall of the yard, looking for deer or fox in the field that lay beyond. He'd been told you could sometimes see wildlife out there, but as far as Dunne could tell the whole terrain had been converted into something muddy and grey and monochromatic.

He felt a tap on his shoulder and he turned.

"Why are you here?" said David Mann.

"Same reason as you."

"I'm here to fight this war."

"Well then there's your answer."

David flushed. "I thought you were shell-shocked. I thought they wouldn't let you back in."

"I thought you were seventeen."

"I'll ask you one more time. What's your reason for coming?"

"In my life, I've rarely had good reasons for doing anything. Believe me when I say it's been a problem."

"Sarah sent you, didn't she?"

"Leave Sarah out of this."

"She thinks I can't take care of myself."

"You're going to find out something soon, kid. There's no protecting people, in battle or out. Doesn't work that way. At first there's quiet and then there's artillery and then all anyone can do is pray that gas doesn't come too, and it was always my impression praying didn't do a whole lot of good anyway."

"You're a liar," said David Mann.

"Among other things, yeah."

This answer infuriated David and he walked away with his hands jammed into his pockets and his shoulders hunched. Yet this interaction, however antagonistic, seemed to narrow the distance between the two men. The next day, Dunne was huddled with Highway, Cahill, Witchell, Johnson and Horne. David Mann walked past them, spurring the Sarcee to play dumb and say, "Hey! There's that other kid from the 10th. Hey, kid, c'mon over."

David did and when Highway introduced the two of them, Dunne said, "We know each other."

"How 'bout that," said Highway. "How 'bout that."

At lunch the next day, David sat with Highway and the others, though he made sure he positioned himself at the opposite end of the table from Dunne. When the meal was over—a sloppy pork gruel they all referred to as "shit on a shingle"— they all lit cigarettes and commiserated.

"At least the milk isn't powdered," said Highway.

"And I've no problem with the peaches in syrup," said Cahill.

"Yeah," agreed Johnson. "They were lovely, them."

"Yeah," said another. "They were."

Another two days passed. Dunne thought often of Sarah and he started two or three letters a day, though each one he balled up and threw away, there being no sane words to describe the reasons why he had left. This inability made him feel like the crazy person he knew himself to be, and with time he decided he preferred to stop thinking about it altogether.

One afternoon, he was in a group with Highway and Horne and some French Canadians he had trouble understanding when an enlistee came up behind him. Dunne had been at the hospital for two and a half weeks, and was beginning to suffer from the same bored, strangulating frustration that everyone there complained of.

"You Michael MacCrae?" asked the Highlander.

"I am."

"You want to come with me?"

"Why would I wanna do that?"

"No reason," said the soldier. "Still, my advice is you do it anyway."

Dunne smirked and followed the guy into the hospital. He wandered past the lobby toward a series of rooms where the CEF officers had set up a row of offices. They entered one of these rooms; three officers, including a colonel whom he knew to be named Ormond, were waiting for him. Ormond was sitting at a large oak desk, and the other two—a major and a lieutenant whom he didn't know—were standing to his left. Military plans were spread across the table.

Dunne saluted.

"Sit," said Ormond.

"Sir," said Dunne, and he lowered himself into the chair facing the colonel.

"Private MacCrae, is it?" asked one of the standing officers.

"Yes sir."

There was an uncomfortable silence. Colonel Ormond next spoke: "I have here a telegram from a Major Dobson-Hughes from the 10th Battalion Recruitment Office. You know him, I believe."

"I do."

"I'll be succinct. Your name is Michael Dunne. You have been awarded the DCM, pursuant to your actions in a small village in the Arras sector. I have this correct?"

Dunne breathed as though wounded. "You do."

"Following the events of that day, however, you deserted and were found wandering with a bullet in your thigh."

"That is accurate, sir."

"So you simultaneously faced recommendation *and* discipline by the army. This is highly irregular, sergeant."

"I know it."

"Then you were found to be suffering from, er—neurasthenia, is it?—and rendered unfit for a return to duty."

"I was."

"And yet, here you are, answering to the name MacCrae. You can imagine how I might find that all a little strange."

Dunne stared straight ahead.

"Could you explain why that is, Dunne?"

"I felt I wasn't done here, sir. It's the best way I can explain it."

Ormond's eyes traced up and down, as though looking for something that might explain his behaviour. "I will tell you this, sergeant. Major Bingham and Lieutenant Hanson both feel I should turn you in to the military authorities. They both share my opinion that this is what you deserve."

"I understand, sir."

"I will also tell you that at this juncture in the war, the concept of *deserve* no longer has much to do with the decisions I make. We are knee-deep in hell, and Currie's projecting sixteen thousand casualties during the next few days alone. The general's never wrong, so I need soldiers and more than that

I need unit leaders. I'm not sure I can count on you, but assurances are another luxury I'm learning to forgo. Do you understand me, soldier?"

"I'm not sure that I do, sir."

"I'm reinstating you as sergeant. You'll lead your old section."

"Respectfully sir, last time I did that people got killed."

"Last time you did that, soldier, a lot of them lived."

Dunne was speechless. Ormond gestured toward the map on his desk.

"This party we call Passchendaele started three months ago and the whole thing's stalled so the job of breaking out falls to the only outfit in this entire circus that seems capable of getting anything done and that's us, the Canadian Expeditionary Force. You know they invented a word for us? The enemy?"

"What is that, sir?"

"They call us the 'storm troopers.' Major Bingham?"

"The assault has two thrusts," said the major. "On the right, brigades from 2nd Division will move up and clear the village. On the left, the Little Black Devils and the 7th Battalion, with us in support, will attack along the Mosselmarkt-Meetcheele Road."

He gestured toward the map with a chubby, dark finger.

"This is the assault front; this is our support line; and this is battalion headquarters. There is also a clearing station for the wounded, as you can see, and a ruined house where command will set up. We have three objectives: Venture Farm, Vindictive Crossroads and One Tree Hill. You'll recognize it. There's a hill and there's a tree. That's where we drop and dig in. Your unit, along with others, will take a section specified here."

The major handed Dunne a file.

"There are your orders. There are maps as well though don't trust them. The landmarks keep getting blown up. Dig in where it says to do so."

"Any questions?" asked the colonel.

"Method of transport, sir?"

"We walk, sergeant. Dismissed."

Dunne saluted and turned and moved from the door. He was about to step back into the hallway when the colonel called out.

"Sergeant?"

Dunne turned. "Sir?"

"You do understand that *this* is your punishment?"

"I understand that, colonel."

ORMOND AND THE OTHER TWO OFFICERS briefed
the unit leaders all day. The following morning,
the soldiers billeting at the hospital for the criminally insane set out, their provisions and weapons
strapped to their backs. It was a misty day, the
clouds above like shredded steel wool. A crumbling and potholed road led northeast, and at the
end of that first long day, all of the men camped on
farmland that had seen better times. There were
more than two hundred men and still the farmer,
a Belgian named Jacques, managed to bring them
enough fresh eggs and milk for everybody, along
with trays of a plum-coloured dessert bread that
his wife spent all day making. He also gave them
handshakes and good wishes in Flemish. They all
went to bed early and woke with the roosters.

They began walking in darkness. By the time
the sun was fully visible in the eastern sky, the road
had petered to nothing; it had been bombed so
often and so thoroughly that the water lying just
two feet beneath it had risen up and submersed
the route in a mixture of mud and brackish water.
Those servicemen who had heard they would be
fighting wet were now realizing that this was not,
in any way, an exaggeration; Dunne heard more
than one stop and scratch his head and say, *Jesus
Christ. It's a bog, not a battlefield.*

The unit commanders, meanwhile, stood looking

at their maps, before concluding that they'd been rendered useless by flooding and bombs. From the near distance, everyone could hear mortar rounds and rifle fire and it was this, coupled with the smell of chlorine rising from the sodden earth, that made it hard to think. Dunne looked over the foggy, flooded landscape. The only things approaching solid earth were naturally formed dykes, which spanned and curved in every direction, not unlike the striations of a leaf. Already, the various units were picking risen walkways and striking out, hoping for the best. Dunne and his men did so as well, finding themselves traversing a muddy pathway with another two units. By midmorning, the path on which they were trudging had diverged into two on a number of occasions, and each time Dunne had had to pick the path that he felt might have the best chance of reaching the village of Passchendaele. Often, he consulted Highway, who had a good sense of direction. Dunne needed this; they'd had reports that many of the dykes ended in water or curved back around so slowly that it was easy to suddenly find yourself walking back where you'd begun. The younger battalion members, including a sullen-looking David Mann, would look on as Dunne and Highway pointed and argued.

By mid-afternoon, Dunne and the eight soldiers under his direct command were alone on a muddy ridge, though occasionally they would spot the hazy outlines of another small group, traversing a dyke far off in the distance; occasionally they'd shine a lantern through the fog and, upon receiving a blinking response, feel less abandoned. It was slow going. With time their path turned to thick mud, surrounded on either side by dirty water. They passed the occasional corpse, turned fish-belly white and bloated with water, and this had a dismaying effect on everyone but the men like Dunne and Highway, who had seen this many times before. David and the younger recruits stopped chatting to one another, adding another layer of solemnity to the journey.

Toward the end of the day, the serviceman named Witchell let out a yelp. Dunne turned and, peering through the mist, saw what looked like a low-lying shrub, gesturing with its branches.

Horne came up. "It's Witchell, sir."

"Yeah?"

"Stuck in the mud."

"Jesus."

"Says he's sinking."

Dunne came a little closer and saw that it was true; the soldier had stepped in a crater that had filled in with an ooze made of soil and water and clay loosened by mortar attack. Witchell was now completely still, his arms stretched out beside him, staring up at the roiling skies. His eyes betrayed his panic.

Though it took a few minutes, Dunne dispatched his men to find a thick, sturdy branch; this was difficult, for most of the trees around them were completely denuded or surrounded by water and impossible to reach. Finally, Johnson came running up with one.

"Lie down," said Dunne.

"What?"

"Down," said Dunne, and the soldier lay flat on his face in the sulphurous mud, the branch held out. Witchell took it with words of thanks. The others grabbed Johnson by the ankles and pulled and in this way they slowly extracted Witchell from the mire, though not before two others had slipped and fallen, which had the effect of kicking mud onto the men still standing. By the time they were finished, every one of them, including Dunne, was either splattered with mud or covered head to toe with it. This had a demoralizing effect on the soldiers. A few hundred yards along the dyke they came upon a cluster of rocks poking through the mud. Here, they all sat and lit cigarettes and stared mournfully at their feet. David looked pale and exhausted and determined not to complain. When the men began collecting their kits, Dunne told them not to hurry, that the war would still be there and they could have another smoke if they wanted.

Every few minutes, the skies lit with tracer flares or outright explosions, and while this only discouraged his men, it helped Dunne, for in the sudden illumination he and Highway would survey the landscape and decide whether they were still marching in the proper direction. Often they weren't, information that Dunne and Highway kept to themselves.

They'd been given a day to reach the front, though Dunne now knew it would take them much longer. At night, they stopped at abandoned farmhouses and cooked dinner over wood fires built in half-collapsed kitchens. They survived on rations and boiled water mixed with chicory. At one old farm they came across a piglet that must have hidden when the farmers had decamped; they found it, frightened and shivering, under the porch, and when all of their efforts failed to extract it, Dunne pointed his rifle through the slats in the steps and shot it in the head. That night, Godin improvised a spit and then scrounged around in the damaged kitchen for seasonings and salt. The skin crackled as it cooked, and inside was the most succulent flesh that Dunne had ever tasted.

They left full-bellied and energized, though the

discovery of the pig turned out to be a mixed blessing: the next night, when they had only rations and a few blackened turnips found in an abandoned root cellar, a mood of loneliness and despair came over the men. Often at night David told the men what they were seeing when they looked up at the darkened sky, but on that night he said little. Before they left the next morning, he wandered away from the group. Dunne followed after him. When he caught up to David he was sitting on the trunk of a felled tree, scribbling something in a notebook.

Dunne sat beside him and for the longest time said nothing.

"Writing Cassie?" he finally asked.

"Yeah," said David. "Figured I should."

David reached into the breast pocket of his jacket and produced the St. George medal. "Cassie gave me this."

"You're lucky."

"She makes me crazy thinking about her."

"Women are like that."

"You written my sister yet?"

"Started to. A couple times. Never managed to finish one."

"You going to tell me why?"

"If I thought it was any of your concern, I would."

"I might just throw this one away too."

"Maybe you and me aren't so different."

David looked up and his eyes burned into Dunne's.

"Yeah," he said." We are."

THEIR LOCATION FINALLY CAME INTO VIEW in the middle of that day's trek, Dunne pointing at what looked to be the aid station and the command house and the mud fields separating the Allies from the enemy. The other men nodded and Highway had just finished saying, "A half-mile at the most," when they all heard a sharp whizzing, and then the ground shook with an explosion that reverberated through the spine and caused a sharp, sudden ache to come to the back, shoulders and neck. They all went down. As they clung to the earth, soil rained upon them. They could smell cordite and their own nervous sweat.

"Stay down!" Dunne yelled, though he was pretty sure he hadn't been heard, for he imagined the others were as deafened as he was. When the explosion finally died away, he lifted his face from the mud and yelled again, "Stay down!"

A voice came to him.

"It's Miles, sir. He's injured."

From far off there was yelling and more artillery and Dunne had to listen keenly through his ringing ears. He heard a high, weak moaning, and he was flooded with both misgivings and the hateful excitement that accompanies battle.

"Anyone else hurt?" Dunne called, and when he did not receive an answer Highway yelled the same question louder: "Is anyone else hurt?" and when the rest of the soldiers sounded off—"No sir. No sir. No sir"—Dunne caught himself listening most closely for David's voice.

Dunne crawled through the mud, his movements guided by Miles's wailing, which he noted was growing weaker and weaker. By the time he reached Miles, the others were there as well, and he could plainly see that a whizz-bang fragment had torn a furrow through Miles's shoulder and upper chest, and that if he lived it would not be in the same way as before the explosion.

"I'll carry him, sir."

It was Johnson who spoke. Dunne nodded, for Johnson was the biggest of them all and would likely be able to move the fastest with the full weight of a man over his shoulders.

"It'll hurt him when you lift him."

"I know it."

Dunne pointed. Off in the distance was a large burlap tent that was busy with men carrying stretchers.

"You think you can get to the clearing station?"

"I do, sir."

Dunne paused and looked in every direction, and he realized that if they were to move Miles it would be best to do so immediately, when the air was still dense with smoke and kicked-up fountains of earth and mud. He nodded. Johnson rose and, with a single clean movement, lifted Miles over rounded shoulders. Miles shrieked and they all ran for the aid station, and when a shell landed on the far side of the station they all flinched and prayed and kept going. They entered the station and Dunne yelled that they needed a medic, for Miles was moaning and clutching himself and yelling that he was going to die, which in Dunne's mind was probably accurate. It was after Johnson had laid Miles on a stretcher that Dunne looked toward the far end of the tent and saw her, looking back at him, her eyes moist, her mouth half-open, her nurse's smock reddened with the effluent of wounds.

THREE

S HE CLOSED HER EYES AND SWALLOWED. When she looked again he was still there—he was not a ghost or a product of her own wishful imagination—and her heart was pounding and he was crossing the floor toward her and as he came closer the scent of him reached her and she again felt as though she'd tumbled into a waking dream.

He stopped before reaching her; she understood that if anyone was watching they would notice that he was standing a little too close. His eyes bore into hers. Her mouth became dry and she felt herself tremble and she wanted nothing more than to touch his tunic, his face, his hands.

"Michael."

"What are you doing here?"

"Where else was I going to go?"

"But *here*? Jesus, Sarah … when did you get here?"

"Maybe a week ago. I volunteered in Saskatoon. They hadn't heard of me there. I almost died when I got your letter."

"I'm sorry."

She said nothing. She continued peering into his eyes, concentrating on the left and then the right and then she counted the lines radiating from either corner and she would have told him she loved him but she knew that the moment the words came from her mouth she would crumble, right here, right in front of the other soldiers and the wounded and the other nursing sisters.

"I can't believe you did that," she said. "Running away without saying goodbye."

"I figured I'd lose my nerve."

"I know why you did it too."

"Turns out you were wrong. David's doing just fine all on his own."

"This had nothing to do with David. You wanted to come back. You used him as your excuse."

At this Dunne said nothing.

"So he's here?" Sarah asked. "My brother?"

"He is."

"And he's all right?"

"He is. He doesn't like what he's seeing, and he's figuring out this isn't what he thought he'd signed up for. But he's dealing with it about as well as you could hope."

She put her hand to her mouth and she closed her eyes with relief. "I wish we could walk away from this. I wish none of this was happening. I wish you and I could go away from here."

"I know, Sarah."

"Tell me again David's okay."

"He is. I'll tell him you want to see him."

"When do they send you out?"

"Likely in the morning. I can't see a reason they'd keep us hanging around."

"You'll be digging trenches."

"I will. David too."

"It'll be dangerous."

"It won't. They're just reserve lines. We're a support company and nothing more. In a few weeks we'll be done and I'll be through here again."

Her eyes filled with tears; she prayed that no one would notice. She lowered her voice to a whisper. "Listen to me."

"I am."

"There's a ruined stone shed a few hundred yards behind us. Meet me there tonight."

"What time?"

"Nine o'clock."

"Does anyone else use it?"

"No one," she said. "It's a ruin."

WHEN ONE OF THE NURSING SISTERS gave her an order, or one of the wounded asked her for something, it was as though they were speaking from a place far off, their voices muffled and coming to her through a tube. Her legs felt jellied, as though made of aspic. There were times when she was overcome with the feeling that she couldn't breathe—she had to sit and fan herself—and at other times her heart would speed, as fast as was possible without breaking, and it was during such moments that the temptation to disappear into the fog caused by a morphine tablet was its greatest.

She'd be dressing a wound or emptying a bedpan or securing a tourniquet and his name would appear in her mind's eye, flashing like a marquee, *Michael Dunne Michael Dunne Michael Dunne,* and she would catch herself staring straight into space, saying nothing, doing nothing, just staring. Late that afternoon, just before rations, a

5.9 artillery shell landed in a forward trench just west of the village. The aid station was overrun with casualties, and when the station was full the wounded were laid out on stretchers outside, in the cold early-November air, all of them screaming or moaning or calling out the names of loved ones. In the middle of this rush, Sarah was frantically cleaning out glasses when she broke one and it cut the top of her left index finger. She just stood there, watching herself bleed into the sink, when the frustration and the pain and the marvel of the past few months finally bubbled up and she started weeping, her tears rolling off her cheeks and mixing with soapy water. One of the other nurses saw this and came over, and bandaged the wound while comforting her.

"There there," she kept saying. "It's just a small wound. Nothing to cry over."

"I'm not crying about my hand."

"I know that, dear. But this little cut is permitting you to cry about the things that really *are* bothering you, and in that way your cut should be viewed as a blessing, don't you think?"

Sarah went outside and smoked a cigarette. She spent the last hour or two of her shift as though in a trance.

Michael Dunne Michael Dunne Michael Dunne …

Her replacement finally came, a wiry thing from Saint Boniface named Laura. Sarah went to the nurses' quarters in the rear of the tent. She changed into a forest-green dress and put on lipstick and eye makeup. When one of the nursing sisters saw her doing this, the woman smiled and looked away.

Sarah rushed through chilled air, making sure she kept to the duck walks. She was carrying a lantern, which she lit when she entered the shed, the flame low and orange and warm. She looked around the shed and wished he were there. She leaned against a table that, she thought, a farmer's wife had once used to pot flowers. There were old hoses piled up in one corner, and a trace used to link a wagon and horse, and in another corner a jumble of old tractor parts, and then he was there, latching the heavy wooden door behind him, and he was coming to her and pressing himself against her and kissing her and she felt as though everything that she'd ever done in her life, every last thing, was fine and allowable, for it had led her here.

He was kissing her neck and ear and cheek, and then she felt his hands inside her blouse, and to help him her trembling hands found her buttons and she fought with them herself, and then his hands, those strong yet gentle sandpaper hands, roamed over her skin and he found the hem of her dress and he yanked it over her hips and she widened her legs and then she had him inside her, inside her thoughts and her soul and her veins, and far off mortar rounds were erupting and there was yelling and the sound of boots stepping through mud, and he was still melding with her and his hands were gripped tight around her forearms, and there was a cracked window on one side of the shed and as she gasped the window lit up with the flash of bombs igniting in the depthless black Belgian sky and it seemed that the rhythm of these flashes matched the rhythms they were setting for themselves and the bombs started erupting faster now, the whole world an eruption of pain, and she dug her teeth into his shoulder and her nails into his arms and she wished for the world and its miseries to end at that cataclysmic moment.

They collapsed together, half-lying and half-sitting on the rickety old potting table. Their breath came in ragged gasps. A minute later, the barrage ended outside; suddenly they could hear wind and bugs chirping. She could also hear her own desperate and hopeful thoughts, swirling in her ears. She gritted her teeth against them and thought, No, no, this will not happen. I will not imagine a future for us.

She took a deep, shuddering breath.

I simply will not.

FOUR

Dunne's section bivouacked that night in a lean-to extending from the house used by the officers. The next morning, they awoke to heavy mist that by eight o'clock had been blown free by cold, northern air. This was replaced by a cloud formation that, over the following hour, turned from grey to gold-brown to black. By nine o'clock, the clouds had opened and the deluge started.

David stood at the edge of the lean-to watching rain pelt the soggy, churned black earth. For the last three days his heart had felt heavy and he felt a painful constriction at the base of his throat; he hadn't thought it would be like this. The same went for Cahill, Godin and Horne. He knew this because they had talked about it, late at night, while warming their hands over low, pale-blue fires. They had pictured adventure, conquest, French-speaking girls, at the very least bread sticks and wine and coffee served in tiny cups that made you feel as though a battery charger had been connected to your heart. Instead, they had become ill on a sickening ocean voyage, had languished for two weeks in a Belgian nuthouse and had walked for days through mud and bad weather, and now word had come that they had lost Miles. He was lonely and depressed, and he pined for Cassie even though he knew he shouldn't. He felt defeated, and it worried him that he hadn't yet laid eyes on a single Hun.

With the rain so heavy they took their time eating. Since the night they'd found the piglet, Godin had more or less assigned himself the role of cook. That morning, a supply runner had arrived on horseback and they were given a handful of eggs, which Godin used to make omelettes fried in lard. They took their time cleaning up too, though after a while the rain penetrated the tarp above them and several leaks opened up and they all suffered water dripping down the backs of their necks.

Other units were leaving. Dunne, who was all

but silent that morning, came to the same decision by about ten o'clock.

"This rain's here to stay."

They all groaned and donned their overcoats and helmets. They put their packs on their backs and, once again, started walking; everyone leaned forward, slightly, to counter the weight hanging from their shoulders. Though the terrain was even muddier than before, this close to the front everything was connected by a series of wooden duck walks, and this made the going a little easier. (Though heaven help the soldier who got distracted by something and stepped off the planks.) Within minutes they were soaked to the skin and shivering; David's boots filled and his underwear was damp and he worried about foot rot, which apparently caused your feet to swell and turn black and poison the rest of the body.

They kept walking. When each man became hungry, he reached into his pack and took dry rations and ate them on the move. Off in the distance there were oak trees, though they'd been torched during previous battles, giving them the appearance of blackened, limbless sentinels. Later that day they passed a village that had been taken by the Germans, only to be regained afterwards by the British. David had never seen anything like it: every building, home, wall or well was at least partially knocked down, and the parts left standing were scrawled with the words *Gott Strafe England* (which, as David was told, meant "May God Punish England.")

The rain was still teeming and David noticed bright red poppies growing in the earth between ruined buildings and this cheered him for a moment only. As they stood in the town square, a dozen or so soldiers walked by in a line, each one wearing bandages around his eyes.

"Gas," said Johnson, and he was right. Each blinded soldier had his hands on the shoulders of the man in front of him, just to know where he was going. The man in the front was sighted, and no older than David, and it was his job to lead these men along the duck walks to the clearance station where Sarah was working. Meanwhile, Dunne studied the map, showing it more than once to Highway. Through teeming rain, David watched them decide on a direction—they both pointed to a road leading from the northeast corner of the square—and then Dunne headed in that direction. The rest of the men glanced at one another, and when Highway fell in line they did so as well. They walked. After a time the duck walk turned into a high-ground path that led through a glade that everyone, apparently, referred to as Dead Forest; Godin and Horne dared to leave the path to collect blackberries and although everyone else yelled at them to hurry no one had a problem with stopping to eat the berries when the two men returned. The forest petered out and the pathway through it turned, once again, into duck walk. At the edge of the woods, they all stopped and looked out at the front for the first time: it was a field of mud and corpses and collapsed wells, and everything, even in the pouring rain, smelled like death. The trenches had been overrun so many times the entire field looked churned, as though it had been subjected to a massive, vindictive plow. Off in the distance, they could see the first of the other trench-building squadrons, digging in the abominable weather.

They walked on. It was more difficult now, for the duck walk had been breached, and there were spots where they had to traverse pure mud; this was dangerous and slow-going and filthy. Whenever they passed other units, they felt slightly better, for it meant they were not alone. After a time, Dunne turned a little to his left and, map in hand, followed his way around a huge muddy rise. They kept going, and David would have wept had others not been there to see him, and finally Dunne stopped in the middle of a sopping, churned nothingness. It was close to nine o'clock at night; digging trenches near the front was possible only under the cover of darkness. He turned to face the others. Rain dripped off his nose and chin.

"This is it."

"What is?" said Witchell.

"Our goddamn trench. Now string out."

They kept low while they waited for supply runners. Within an hour a pair of soldiers arrived and dropped a pile of small shovels in the wet earth. They left without a word. David took one and found a spot about two-thirds of the way along their section. Cahill was a couple of yards to his right and the big man, Johnson, was a couple of yards to his left. David started digging, and like Cahill and Johnson he cursed the size of his instrument—it was a small, pointed spade, much like the type used for camping. Soon David's hands felt calloused, and his back hurt from bending so far over to lift the heavy, dripping earth.

A trough quickly formed, though as it did the water table beneath them seeped into the bottom, such that liquid now came at them from above and from below. They had to stop when the trench was no more than three feet deep; any farther and cold water gushed up and filled more than they had unearthed. This demoralized them further. Occasionally, there was a mammoth concussive boom that shook the ground and caused black, dripping mud to slide away from the sides of their trench. At the same time, the sky to the northwest would cascade with a strobing, blue-white intensity. Whenever this happened, they all dropped chest-first into the mud, for in the sudden light they became targets for the German soldiers dug in to the east. It was only when the skies returned to black, and shock waves had stopped ricocheting through their bones, that they rose from the mud.

With time, other units arrived and began digging and soon their section of trench met the ends of the other trenches, forming a long, curving, three-foot ditch that would reach toward the end of the breach. They sat in the mud, exhausted and hungry and soaked through to the skin. They all reached into their kit bags and pulled out lengths of wet sausage and mealy, worm-bitten apples that had been given to them at command. David bit into the food and felt desperate. Everyone tried to sleep, though it was impossible: they were wet and cold and they'd reached the degree of exhaustion whereby the mind fills the ears with an urgent high-pitched whine. Furthermore, the chemicals in the mud were starting to affect them: their eyes stung and their skin itched and their lungs felt as though they were beginning to burn.

In the middle of the night, the supply runners dropped off sandbags. The men set to work in a fever, mounding the bags on the sides of their trenches so they could at least stand up in a crouch with their heads protected from fire. Within a few hours their section of trench was more or less finished, save for lengths of ground sheet that they hoped would show up in the morning. David assumed this was true for the other sections, though he couldn't say for sure—the trench had been built in a long, snaking curve, so that no soldier (or, more to the point, no enemy soldier) could see more than about ten yards along it.

Dawn was still an hour or two away.

David sat and felt uncomfortable when the sergeant sat in mud beside him. They both smoked and looked at the back wall of the ditch. For the longest time they didn't speak.

"This is insane," David finally said.

"It's what you signed up for."

"I signed up to kill Germans."

"I reckoned you signed up to kill your father."

David said nothing, resenting that Dunne knew things about him that he'd thought were hidden, far beneath the surface, away from all eyes or questions or thought. Dunne spoke.

"You tell me somethin', soldier."

"What's that?"

"You still mad at me for not signing you up?"

David thought about this. He thought about the wet and the cold and the bloated dead bodies he'd seen on the way to the front and the signs reading *May God Punish England* and the collapsed villages. Worst of all, he thought about the twelve men blinded by gas, trying to feel their way along the duck walks.

He also thought about Cassie.

"Yeah," he answered. "A little."

"Good," said Dunne. "Keep it that way."

There was a sparking of weak light above them. David looked up; a string of stars peered through a break in the ink-black clouds.

"What do you know?" Dunne said. "A patch of sky."

"It's Fornax."

"What is?"

"That constellation."

"Yeah?"

"It's the furnace. It's where things burn."

"I thought that was here."

They chuckled grimly and for some reason David felt good for doing so. Dunne settled against the mud wall and folded his arms over his stomach and closed his eyes.

"Get some sleep, soldier. This peace and quiet won't last."

FIVE

HERE, SITTING UPRIGHT IN MUDDY WATER, in a frigid supply trench, beneath a mash of dark rustling clouds, his coat pulled tight at his neck, the night air infected with a faint reek of phosgene and gunpowder and decomposition, his leaking boots sloshing in cold and vermin-plagued waters (and if he wasn't mistaken there was a corpse about thirty yards beyond them, bloated and waterlogged and with rats feasting at its eyes) ... here, near the Belgian village of Passchendaele, in the most active section of the Western Front, the sergeant had no trouble sleeping. He only had to tip his head back, so that the top of his helmet grazed the sandbag wall he'd made himself that night, and he fell into an achy, thickened dream. It was one that he had often: he was no more than seventeen, in some small town in Alberta, Fort Macleod probably, and he'd drawn the meanest bull, a ton and a half of hellfire named Jackson, and he was frightened because of it. The chute opened and he held on and the bull left-twisted like an unleashing of dynamite, and before he knew it he'd hit the ground hard, and it was then that the whole of the world stopped—he'd fallen in the bad spot, behind the bull and a little to the left, and meanwhile his right foot had somehow become entangled in one of the lariats surrounding the animal's torso. He wasn't going anywhere, and the bull only had to twist, dig down with his horns and kill his rider. Dunne watched it happen as though in a series of snapshots: the bull turned, and in his fury to kill he glanced the ground with his horns just a little too early, tearing Dunne's jeans as he knifed his horns into the air. The bull's feet left the ground and he twisted in the air, and when the bull landed he became enraged with one of the clowns and left his rider to live. Dunne lay in red rodeo earth, ribs broken, collarbone like a twist of tobacco, right ankle mangled, looking at a chunky Albertan sky, and he had an absurd momentary feeling that all events occur for a reason, that all things in the universe are somehow connected, and that the hand that connects these things is a kind one. It was a feeling that resided far off in the corner of his thinking, however, and it vanished the moment he turned his attention to it.

He could still remember how it felt, though.

DUNNE WAS AWOKEN by the whistle of the first tracers. Shortly thereafter, the day rose hazy and cold; above him, Dunne could see kestrels and wisps of spent grey cloud. It started raining, and each time a flare lit up the sky, he watched rain dance upon the water pooled in the bottom of the trench, like little dancers turned a blazing chalk-white blue. Within a moment, he heard German artillery start up—trench mortars, field artillery, machine guns—and the air filled with explosives and bullets and the roasting stench of cordite. The return fire followed immediately after, and there was nothing to do but sit and wait and listen to the battle being waged at the front. Some of the soldiers plugged their ears, but Dunne didn't because there was something to be said for letting your ears deafen as soon as possible—otherwise, they had a way of going on you when you most needed them and were still in the bad habit of depending on them. He kept checking the gas mask hanging around his neck. Though this accomplished nothing, he, like every other soldier, knew that mud could clog the filter, meaning that your mask suffocated you instead of letting you breathe. He dug at the filter with his thumb.

The explosions went on. After a time Cahill came around the corner and squatted in the stinging, chemical mud next to Dunne. He waited for a break in the fire and when none came he yelled into Dunne's ear.

"What's it look like, sarge?"

Dunne shrugged. "I dunno," he yelled.

"They gonna need us?"

"Too early to tell's what I figure."

"So we wait?"

"We wait."

Cahill began to say something else, some theory about why or why not they'd be called to relieve the Devils at the front, though it was too loud and Dunne could only hear every third or fourth word, and then a shell landed close enough that the resulting smoke drifted into their section of the trench and clung to the wet on their faces and caused their eyes to tear. Both Cahill and David Mann moved for their masks, though they stopped when they realized that the backs of their throats weren't burning.

"Just smoke," Dunne yelled. "Just goddamn smoke."

Cahill nodded and punched Dunne on the shoulder and moved off. Judging by the explosions emanating from the battle site, the artillery was mostly Howitzer fire. This made Dunne feel somewhat secure in their position, though he could tell that the odd mortar round was being shot up as well and that was where the majority of his concerns lay. He kept peering through a peephole he'd built into the sandbags; all he could see was rain and black earth and a smouldering graphite-coloured smoke and, occasionally, darting through it, a set of panicked legs.

He sat back on the fire step and looked at David Mann and said, "I'm gonna go see what's happening. Stay here."

David nodded and Dunne ran bent over around the slowly curving trench the various units had looped together earlier. These units formed the majority of Platoon 2, and Dunne wanted to see what other command was in place and what the thinking was. It was difficult; as the trench curved toward the east, the Howitzer shells created more of a concussion and each time one went off the earth rocked and Dunne fell more than once. At one point, he passed what he thought was a communications officer, though when he moved to salute he realized it was just another kid soldier who happened to be near a wireless telephone.

Dunne leaned close to the kid's ear and yelled, "Has there been any communication?"

"Sir?" the soldier yelled back, a hand cupped around his ear.

"Have you heard anything?"

"Sir?"

"*You heard anything?*"

"Telephone's dead, sir."

"Dead?"

"Sir?"

"Why?"

"I beg your ..."

Dunne shook his head and gave up and moved farther along the trench, careful to keep his head low and his back stooped and his footfalls near the sides of the trench, where the water hadn't pooled so deep. He noticed that the soldiers in this part were not sitting patiently for orders as his men were, but running and screaming and in some cases weeping, and he turned a corner and it was then he saw why. A mortar shell, lobbed high into the tracer-lit sky, had landed so close to the final northern section of the line it must have felt as though the world had ended. A blanket of casu-

alties had formed in the rain, and the injured—
men newly one-armed, or blinded, or bleeding to
death—scampered like panicked children across
the backs of the men who had fallen. The Huns,
meanwhile, had spotted the explosion and deduced
that they'd got lucky and were now directing much
of their fire over the heads of the forward soldiers
toward that part of the supply trench; though the
Germans were far away, it was enough to give the
stretcher bearers something to think about. With
the mud and the confusion, their progress was
close to nonexistent.

Dunne moved away as quickly as he could
without losing his footing. He arrived back panting and gathered the others.

"They've hit the trench," he told them over the
roar of artillery.

"Where?" Johnson yelled.

"At the end. Did some real damage."

"How real?" someone else yelled.

"*Real*," hollered Dunne, and he looked over
and saw that David was shaking.

"It's all right," Dunne yelled. "Just sit tight.
Here, we're safe. Here, we're …"

He suddenly went hoarse and lost his voice
and then it was a matter of shutting up, for even
the greenest of privates could figure out that if
the enemy was managing to attack the rearmost

trenches then those soldiers might as well be under attack at the front, where at least they could fight back. They all waited. The wind lifted and the rains fell in chilled sheets; Dunne's men sat back and felt miserable and watched the rotating, insect-swarm patterns these sheets formed in the air. The enemy, with its success down the line, began sending up more shell-fire, and each time one landed there was a loud, thumping concussion that caused slides of mud to slip away from the sides of their shallow, makeshift trench. A second later, smoke would drift over them and mix with rain and turn to something that looked like a drifting, airborne soup.

The pounding went on and it was impossible to talk and so they did nothing but stare miserably at the splattering mud floor. Some, Dunne noticed, pulled out pictures of loved ones and risked exposing them to the rain and others turned St. Christopher medals in their fingertips and others closed their eyes and moved their lips and Dunne knew they were praying. He watched as David reached a shaky hand into his pocket and pulled out the St. George medal. David kissed it and wound it tightly around the fingers of his left hand so that the medal was facing him; he then watched it bead with cold rain.

The noise of the barrage suddenly reduced by about half. The men stopped what they were doing and looked up, as if the reason for this reduction in volume could be found in the rain-drenched skies. Some even smiled, not realizing it was the Allied return fire that had vanished.

Highway came beetling through the mud and stood crouched before the sergeant.

"What the fuck?"

"I dunno."

"What happened to our fire?"

"I dunno."

"Can't be good."

Dunne felt David's eyes upon him so he didn't respond. Highway realized that no answer was coming so he asked another question.

"What did the other command think when you went down the trench?"

"Couldn't find any."

Highway looked at him. "What're you sayin', Mikey?"

"Could be I'm it. It was chaos, there."

Dunne kept checking his wristwatch, and in this way he saw that something strange was happening: time kept lurching forward and then stumbling to an absolute standstill and then whole chunks of it would disappear. It was something he'd noticed in previous battles: the way that the experience departed from all laws of nature, even the passage of time, giving it a feel understandable only to those who have been through it. He breathed deeply.

A runner popped his head over the rear wall of the mud-filled trench. Dunne didn't see him at first, as the runner was directly above him. David did, however, and he pointed to a spot above Dunne's helmet. Dunne turned and looked up and he saw the expression on the runner's face and from farther down the line he could already hear the sound of boots tromping through mud.

"We're going," yelled the runner.

A second later, Dunne and his men were over the sandbag lip and running toward the forward trench.

SIX

THE TABLETS WERE STORED in a large glass jar in a cabinet at the rear of the clearing station, next to flasks containing dressings, bandages, empty hypodermic syringes and wads of cotton batting. Every time Sarah passed the cabinet, she imagined them, in there, all those tablets, resonating light, breathing false promise, and though they were *supposed* to be inventoried the sisters could never quite get it right in Calgary, never mind in the chaos of the front.

The *things* she was seeing.

A young soldier, brought in with superficial

wounds, one of the lucky ones. She tended to him—he needed nothing more than a cool compress and to be told he was okay—though when she moved to leave, a slight hand reached out and took hers and he begged, "Don't leave me, please don't leave me," and she looked down into his eyes and saw a fear that would cripple him severely and forever. "It's okay, hush, I'm right here," she said, and she decided to inject him with something that would put him to sleep for the better part of the day. Yet it was the look in his eyes—a cold abyss, an absolute loss of hope, a realization of what the human soul was capable of—that caused her to think of going to the medicine cabinet and, when none of the sisters were looking, reaching in and taking a tablet.

Or, another young soldier (for they were so often young, with the waist and chest diameters of boys), his toes swollen and turned a blossom of blue and dark red; when the medics came by they chided him for not drying his feet on the hour, or changing his socks three times a day, or rubbing his toes with the whale-oil grease the army had given him *for that exact purpose*. The medic sniffed the toes and tapped them with a reflex hammer and when the young man was informed they would have to come off, that he had an advanced case of trench foot, he pleaded with them—"Oh God, please oh God"—to look for another way.

Or, it happened, it did, the private's wound gaping along the full length of his torso; it was only a matter of time, and this wound was sucking air, like a rubbery pump. It must have been a direct hit, most likely a smaller Howitzer shell; his time on earth was up and the worst of it was that nobody was attending to him, he was a lost cause and their resources were stretched and so he would die alone and unattended. Sarah went to him and she opened her heart and she mustered all the love she had ever felt in her life and she gave it to this young boy so that at least he would not die unloved and his exit from this world would not go unnoticed.

And oh, oh, to reach inside one of those jars, to grab just one small tablet, to swallow it and feel her body turn warm and her feet lift from the ground and all those around her dissolve ...

They were worked mercilessly. There was never a time when she was not running between patients or dressing a wound or prepping a soldier (as well as she was able) for surgery. Day or night, it seemed to Sarah, had become a distinction that no longer applied—the injured never stop coming, it never became light out, it was always dark and wet and hellish. She never imagined it would be this way. A military ambulance arrived, three o'clock in the afternoon (or was that three in the morning?), full of wounded men from the north end of the supply trench, the Huns seemed to have got their mortar range down. The clearing station descended into chaos, soldiers screaming and yelling and crying in panicked soldier voices. Doctors hurled orders at the nurses, either everything was being done or nothing at all, perhaps in the unreality of battle they could coexist, the everything and the nothing, and it was all Sarah could think of, it was the only thing she could picture, the words were constantly on the tip of her tongue ...

That jar, that jar, that jar.

That brimming with beautiful light-blue tablets *jar*.

THERE WAS A CALM. The sounds in the sky diminished and Sarah interpreted this as a good sign. At least half of the wounded who had survived the supply-trench strike had been shipped to a field hospital near the Belgian border. The ones who remained were not so badly off and had been assigned to a later convoy. Or they had died and were being taken away on stretchers, their at-rest expressions covered by dirty white sheets. One of the nurses made a pot of tea, and they all went behind the station and took a break beneath a tarpaulin awning. With their tea, they ate biscuits and smoked cigarettes, even though the latter were unladylike.

The nursing sisters finished up and started going back inside. Sarah found herself with a nurse named Morgan who was not quite as formidable as some of the others.

"What is your name, child?"

"Sarah."

For a moment, Sarah actually thought about telling her the reasons why she had come. She thought about telling her that she had been a nurse at a military hospital in Calgary, but then everyone found out that her father (her petty, vindictive father) had fought for the Germans, and that he had been a drinker, and maybe that's where her weakness for tablets came from—she couldn't say exactly, the world just felt so cold without them—but at any rate she had lost her job, and her brother and the man she had just started loving had both lied their way into the war, and so there was nothing left for her, nothing left for her at all. So she'd taken a bus to Saskatoon, and there, at a recruitment station, she'd run up against an enlistment officer with better things to do than check the service records of every young woman who wanted to join the First

World War medical services, particularly one who was still young (or at least youngish) and was flirtatious that day and had unfastened the top button of her blouse. He'd told her that women like herself were going to be the determining factor in our God-blessed fight with the Huns, and he'd enlisted her without hesitation.

She thought about telling *all* of this to Sister Morgan, and then decided that she barely believed it herself. She took a deep breath and said something she'd heard other young nurses say.

"I came her looking for adventure, I suppose."

"I suspect you weren't prepared for this."

"No, I'm afraid I wasn't."

"Don't worry, Sarah. The times will get better. They always do."

"I know."

"Would you care to pray with me?"

Sarah surprised herself by saying, "Yes, I think that I would."

She lowered her head and, for a time, listened to the nurse mumbling beside her. Soon she found herself adding her own wishes: that her brother would be okay, that Dunne would be okay, that all of this wouldn't prove to be too much for her. When she finished, she lifted her head and listened to the sound made by the rain hitting the canopy of a nearby forest—it was like something small, something with many tiny feet, running over the skin of a drum. She listened some more. You could pick it out from the guns and cannons and the groans of men. After a while, she decided that if this distraction proved to be the only thing she'd accomplished by praying, she would have to conclude that praying worked.

THEY WERE CALLED INSIDE. One of the doctors, a young man with silver hair named McAndrew, was standing next to the supply cabinets at the rear of the tent. He spotted them and waved them over and when Sarah reached the circle of nurses he began.

"We have just received word from Colonel Ormond."

He looked from nurse to nurse.

"The troops in the supply trenches are bolstering the troops in the advance trenches."

Sarah's heart pounded. Two names screamed in her mind. *Dunne, David.*

"Why is that?" asked one of the sisters.

"He wouldn't tell me."

He paused for a moment, as if to convey the importance of what he was saying via silence.

Sarah felt light-headed and weak and cold in her hands and feet. The doctor continued: "But it doesn't take a genius to figure out that something is going to happen, and when it does … well."

He looked down and cleared his throat. "I won't mince words. We can expect casualties to be extensive."

Sarah felt the contents of her stomach rise to her throat, so she ran outside and vomited into a bank of earth turned muddy in the relentless downpour. When she was finished, she wandered back inside; Sister Morgan spotted her and took her arm and lay her on a cot. She put a cool cloth on Sarah's head and asked if she was okay. Sarah thanked her, looking up at the pale-green tarpaulin roof. Guns were still firing and soldiers were still moaning.

"You're white as a ghost."

"I'm sorry."

Later, Sarah rose to her feet and still felt nauseous. She got a glass of sterilized water and again she stepped outside the clearing station. She then walked through drizzle toward the nurses' quarters. Inside, she lay on her bunk and tried not to think about Dunne or David or her own puzzling existence. Evening was falling. Her heart pounded and she felt alone. When everything was dark outside, she rose and tromped along the duck walks separating the nurses' quarters from the aid station. All was quiet, or at least relatively quiet, and Sarah went from bed to bed, offering comfort in any way she could, though her real design was the jar in the supply cabinet; she had planned her rounds to take her past it, in a way that seemed natural and unforced and deserved.

When she reached the cabinet, she stopped and turned her back. Just this once, she thought, anyone would, that's what it's there for, and without looking behind her she reached in and extracted the jar and spun off the lid and took one of the tablets. Just before popping it into her mouth, she turned and saw the young soldier she'd helped earlier that day, the one who had no real wounds to worry about and for that reason couldn't help thinking about the war and the rain and the chemical-soaked mud and his chances of surviving all of it. His eyes were wide open, and even in the gloom of the tent they looked a deep, mournful blue. He knew what she was doing. There wasn't the slightest trace of judgment in his glance, and for some reason this touched Sarah and made her feel embarrassed.

He extended his arm, just slightly, over the edge of the bed. His palm was turned upward. He opened it slowly and Sarah walked over and put the tablet in the boy's hand.

"Don't tell anyone," she said.

He nodded.

"Don't chew it, it's bitter. Just swallow."

"Yes."

She stayed with him until his face shone and his eyes rolled back and he smiled, widely, before saying, "Thank you, nurse," and entering a place that was neither wakeful nor asleep nor in between the two.

SEVEN

THEY KEPT LOW AND MOVED QUICKLY. Nobody spoke; there was a lull in the firing and they could hear nothing but the sucking noise of boots pulling out of mud and their own raspy breathing. It was dawn, the light grey and textured. After a hundred yards, they entered a small forest separating the rearmost trenches from those at the front. The trees were mostly bare and limbless and many had been uprooted by mortar shells so that they ran horizontal along the floor of the forest, their upended roots like giant wooden webs. Here, the mud had turned to a putrescent bog. The soldiers moved from the base of one tree to another, so that the roots of the trees prevented them from sinking into the damp soil. There were few duck walks here, and the ones that remained had mostly snapped or fragmented.

The forest floor was littered with mulching dead leaves and fallen limbs and the bodies of 8th Battalion soldiers who had crawled wounded into the forest for protection and then died, eyes bulging, mouths open, hands grasping for the next root to pull on. The stretcher bearers couldn't operate here, and Dunne was sure he could hear weak moaning, meaning that some of the fallen Devils were alive, though in the low light and the rain he couldn't tell which ones. The effect was ghostly and one he didn't like. He could taste decomposition on the tip of his tongue, like drops of a noxious liquid. He kept hearing men spit, an attempt to rid their mouths of the poisonous stench, and though he knew it wouldn't work he did it himself nonetheless. His eyes burned and though he was tired he felt good; this moment was a long time coming and one he richly deserved.

He came to a break in the forest. Here, he stopped, as did the men behind him. They all peered out in silence. They saw what was left of the front-line trenches, and beyond that was no man's land: mud and smouldering pyres and dead horses and smashed cannons and circling vultures and burnt bits of wagons and splintered mud-digging shovels and the stumps of blackened hollowed-out trees and the odd dropped broken gun and scurrying puppy-sized trench rats and old shredded supply truck tires and spent Howitzer casings with their smoking tips pointing into the mud and runner dogs caught dead in crossfire and, every twenty yards or so, shell craters filled with water and blood and men floating face up and swollen and lifeless.

"Jesus," someone said.

Highway pulled up beside Dunne and said, "Mikey, there's nothing left to defend."

"Can't turn back."

"We could dig in here, wait for reinforcements."

"Here they could sight on the trees. It'd be worse. Flame-throwers would burn us out anyway."

"Not if we shot 'em as they came upon us."

"We have orders."

"This is a helluva time to start worrying about orders."

Dunne's eyes swept the debris and the mud and the wounded all around him. He knew that many of these men would die that day, and that the sins of mankind were of a calibre deserving respect and disgust. He turned. His soldiers had been joined by others from the supply trench—they were maybe sixty in all—and he wondered if he was supposed to be in charge of them too.

"Stay spread out," he hissed. "You got that? Stay spread out."

Some of the men nodded but most just looked exhausted and afraid.

"Everybody ready?"

A few nodded, though most just looked forward, their expressions blank.

"*Go*," said Dunne.

THEY RAN LOW AND FAST OVER THE HELLISH FIELD. The moment they emerged from the forest their ears rang with machine-gun fire, and as Dunne ran through the field he kept hearing the sickening thud of bullets hitting flesh and the gurgled throat-bursts of men who had just been shot. He didn't look back, though at one point he turned to one side and saw David out of the corner of his eye, dodging shell craters and corpses, and then the remains of the trench were close enough that Dunne made a final zigzagging burst and jumped feet-first. He landed in water and moved along the ruins of the trench and as he did he could see that David, Highway, Cahill, Witchell, Godin, Johnson and Horne had made it as well.

Dunne spotted a Lewis gunner who was about to abandon his position. The gunner froze when he saw the approaching sergeant.

"Who's your commander, soldier?"

"Dead, sergeant. All dead. Anyone with a stripe is dead."

The gunner put on his pack and was about to leap over what was left of the rear wall of the trench. Dunne could see that the rest of the 8th Battalion was doing the same.

"Where the hell you going?"

"I've had the shit kicked out of me for eight straight hours."

"You can't leave us strung out here. We're just a small company. Maybe sixty guys."

"You want me to stay, you're gonna have to shoot me."

Dunne pulled out his rifle and aimed it at the gunner's head and he felt his forefinger tremble with the same fury that had bothered him the whole of his life. A 5.9 shell screamed down and landed just feet from where Dunne was about to shoot the gunner, and when it failed to detonate Dunne looked at it, amazed, and in this pause the gunner disappeared over the rear trench facing and was gone.

Highway and Cahill came splashing through the water. Cahill had a pair of binoculars. He handed them to Dunne and gestured over the mess of loosened sandbags topping the lip. Risking fire, Dunne poked his head up and looked; he could see the German bayonets poking out of the trenches, a procession of metal reeds. He also saw that the enemy had fastened two planks together with barbed wire to form a cross and had mounted it just outside of their trench; seeing this, Dunne thought that if they wanted God on their side, then they could have Him. Most likely it was designed to taunt them.

Dunne lowered back down into the trench. Highway spoke.

"They're comin', Mikey. Sure as shit they're comin'."

"They are."

"We don't have enough guys."

"We got what we got. Spread out. Two to a crater. Lewis guns on the flanks."

Word spread and the men who'd made it to the trench spread out and put new ammunition clips into their rifles and levered them through gaps in the sandbags. Everything was quiet now. Dunne settled in next to David.

"You scared?"

"Yeah."

"Good. It'll help. We'll get through this."

Dunne's original men had stayed close, and he could see them down the line, sighting the enemy.

To his right were David, Johnson, Cahill and Horne. To his left were Highway, Godin and Witchell; he saw Witchell move to light a cigarette and when his matches failed he swore and looked defeated. Dunne took his lighter out of his breast pocket and handed it to Highway and then motioned toward Witchell. Highway handed it along.

They waited. Everything turned deathly silent. The sun was rising above the horizon now, though in the rain and the fog everything remained shrouded in a smeary, off-white gloom. When Dunne's lighter was passed back he lit a cigarette as well and let the smoke warm his lungs. He noticed small things. The way the smoke from his cigarette coiled in stubby blue circles. The way the rain beaded for a moment on the sleeve of his tunic, as though trying to decide which way to roll off. In front of his nose, the sprouting of a blood-red poppy, growing between the wooden slats of the parapet.

The sound of his men breathing.

THEY WAITED. Every once in a while Cahill would report that the bayonets in the opposite trench were wavering and that he could hear talking in German and that the assault was seconds away, but then nothing would happen. Time passed. Dunne started to think of past moments of his life—from his boyhood, from the sawmill, from nights spent wandering—and he couldn't help but feel sorry that they came to him so jumbled up, like the flashes of a dream, without a thread or any sort of reason to bind them. He thought of odd things, things that he hadn't thought of in years, and it felt as though someone or something was sending him clues about the meaning of his life so far. When a series of German flares lit up no man's land like a fairground, Dunne felt himself pulled back into the moment, as though yanked airborne through a tube.

"Here it comes," someone said, and it was like the very bones within them were being sawed or cracked or bombarded, and they covered their ears and it didn't matter, for the sound was coming from not only above them and beside them but below them, in the shaking trembling erupting earth, and in this way it travelled up through their legs and their spines and into the part of the mind that generates fear and dementia.

"Get down!" Dunne yelled, and they all covered themselves, for a volley of Howitzer shells was landing in the mud field separating the two enemies, and every time one went off it kicked up spumes of mud and shit and body parts and old dead animals, and they came raining down on Dunne's men like a hellish, slopping punishment. The air was thick with Mauser bullets, and when Horne submitted to temptation and poked his head over the lip of the parapet, he was hit in the face with several bullets at the same time, such that much of what used to be his head landed on the neck and shoulders of Witchell, the soldier next to him, who sat in bloody water and put his face in his hands and screamed, "Oh my fucking god." Horne sank into the mire and, Dunne knew, would quickly be put to use as traction when the fighting really started.

He peered through the aperture in the sandbags and saw them, hundreds of them, the numbers were terrifying, and they were yelling in German as they ran through no man's land in a cover of cannon and machine-gun fire and high-lobbed mortar rounds meant to deafen and confuse.

"Hold on!" Dunne yelled, though he knew that farther down the line they couldn't hear him and were already firing at the Germans, even though they were still too far and the visibility was poor and the trajectory of their bullets and tossed Mills bombs was affected by the numbing fall of rain from the sky.

"Hold on!" Dunne yelled again, and this time Highway heard and he yelled the same thing—"Hold on, goddamn it, hold on!"—and soon this command echoed along the water-filled trench so that everyone, even those who had been shooting, trained their weapons at chest-height and waited with their fingertips trembling. Every nerve in Dunne's body was firing, and when he looked over at David he saw that the muscles in the side of his too-young face twitched and looked spastic. The enemy closed to within fifty yards, and then forty yards, and then thirty-five, and when they were within twenty-five yards Dunne yelled, "Fire!" and the air now flew with bullets from Lewis guns and Lee-Enfield rifles and the enemy charging them started to fall like dropped sacks. Dunne's men reloaded and fired and reloaded and fired and, out on no man's land, limbs flew and helmets dropped and sprays of hot blood mixed with chilled falling rain. They still came, Dunne could not believe how many they were, and when a thick line of grey uniforms was within ten yards he knew for certain that they would not be repelled solely by return fire and grenades. Dunne fired his last round and flipped his rifle and inserted the bayonet. He held it like a club in his right hand. In his left was a trench knife. The others were doing the same, and seconds later the Germans were in the trench and from that moment on it became a pastiche, a psychotic and violent dance. As Dunne fought, he saw Johnson sidestep a German, although the German's bayonet ran through Johnson's hand right up to the barrel and Johnson plunged his knife into the side of the German's head and there was blood and spilled pulpy matter. Dunne heard a whizzing followed by a bang, and then Cahill was standing and talking dazed to himself with one arm missing and he slowly fell into the quagmire. Dunne stabbed a Hun in the throat and screamed, "Come at me! Come at me!" and when they complied he stabbed and ripped and tore while shrieking that they should come and kill him, that they should come and fucking kill him, and he had never felt more alive or out of his own skin, and then Dunne felt a hard shove on his shoulder blades. He fell and rolled and saw a Fritz drawing back to plunge his bayonet into Dunne, and Dunne was trapped between two bodies and was about to die and everything started to make sense when he saw David standing behind the German, and David was chambering a bullet while Dunne yelled, "Shoot, goddamn it, shoot," and the ensuing spray landed hot and pulpy across Dunne's face. He wiped at the muck occluding his vision and saw Witchell feeding a belt of ammunition into Godin's Lewis gun and then Godin opened fire *inside* the trench, and though he necessarily hit a few Canadians the vast majority of those standing were Germans and they were the vast majority of those who fell down dead. The rest saw this and there was yelling and then they were back over the melting trench walls and heading for their own. The Canadians, exhilarated, hopped over the wall and chased them despite Dunne screaming, "No! No! Stay put, goddamn it!"

They mostly didn't listen. *It was their moment.* There was more fighting and more death and when they all came running back into the trench they were exhausted and yelling and laughing and, above all else, soaked through with hot sticky red mucilaginous Fritz blood.

"Form up!" Dunne yelled, and they tightened around him, still giddy and elated and bloody. "Who's dead?"

"Cahill," called Witchell.

"Horne," groaned Johnson, who was bent over and holding his badly wounded hand.

"Two dead?" Dunne yelled, and he looked at his nodding men and then he noticed something. He began to tremble. "Where's Mann?" he yelled.

"He was next to you," Highway said.

Dunne looked up and down the trench while muttering, "Goddamn it, goddamn it," and he set off, staying low, using the backs and fronts of fallen men to stay above the muddy blood-soup beneath him. There was no sign of the kid. He returned to his section of trench and he yelled, once again, "Where the fuck is the kid?" and they all shrugged except for Godin, who was peering through a break in the sandbags and saying, "You better look, sarge, you better look."

EIGHT

*T*HIS WAS THE REASON HE'D SIGNED UP. It was this feeling, this moment, this glory. It was not to appease Cassie's father, not to defend his country, not to be a hero. Oh no. When he was perfectly honest with himself, it was this feeling of invincibility, it was this feeling that he could do anything, it was this feeling of godlike power. He had held the Hun's life in his hands. He and he alone had decided his fate. *He* had loaded the gun without trembling, and he had aimed and he had pulled the trigger, and he had saved another man's life and the dead man had deserved it. He had done *all* of this. He had meted out destiny and judgment. As he'd watched the German soldier fall—the one that had been about to *kill* Michael Dunne—it filled him with a sensation that, he suddenly realized, he'd been searching for his entire life. He no longer cared about Cassie or his problems back home. Why bother, when he was David Mann, a taker of life, a warrior? A lack of direction was a problem that would no longer plague him. He would devote the rest of his life to the pursuit of *this* excitement. He would have any girl he wanted, he would take any job he deigned to take, he would lead any life *he* wanted to lead. He saw that now, saw it as clearly as he'd ever seen anything. It was the reason he'd come here. When the other Canuck soldiers (who no doubt were feeling the same thing he was) hopped over the sandbags and started chasing the retreating Germans over no man's land, it had not been his legs, nor his heart, that had propelled him over the wall. Oh no, it had been that intoxicating feeling, that sure knowledge that he was young and strong and impervious to bullets, and so he had charged while screaming, "Die, you Hun motherfuckers, die!" Up ahead he'd spotted the barbed wire–wrapped cross they'd put up near their trench and this had incensed him further—*How dare they! How dare they!*—and so he'd shot at retreating grey backs and as they fell in his path the feeling had grown more intense, more savage, setting his mind on fire, setting his lungs ablaze, drugging him with a substance causing euphoria, and this feeling had continued to peak, making him feel all the more invincible, making him feel all the more glorious, and then a grenade erupted beside him and another detonated just ahead of him. In that instant, the rage coursing through his body changed to an intense and washing fear, for suddenly the air was grey and filled with smoke and fountaining mud, and then another explosion—this one several times larger—erupted about twenty feet away, sending shock tremors through the earth. David tripped and fell into a crater filled with water and mud and blood and two pale, bloated, bug-ravaged bodies, and when he scrambled out of the hole he lost his rifle somehow and when he looked around his only desire was to make it back to his own trench in a single piece, for he was no longer invincible, and he was no longer going to live forever, and even worse he was lost—lost in this insanity of noise and smoke and mud and men screaming in both German and English so he just ran, hoping for the best, and then he saw it, a lip of sandbags appearing in the gloom, so he ran toward it, bullets flying all around him, and he jumped over the lip and fell into knee-deep water and when he rose he learned about the things that blind panic can make you do.

A German officer was pointing a pistol at him, about to end his young life.

"Please," David called. "Bitte, bitte."

The officer was tall and thin and his eyes were narrow and dark. He smiled, revealing a row of peggy gold teeth, and he slowly lowered the gun from David's chest to David's leg, moving the Luger slowly, slowly. When he fired, a searing white-hot burn travelled from David's thigh to the rest of his body, scorching his feet and his hands and the inner recesses of his stomach and chest. David fell into water, holding himself and screaming, his pain a rushing whitewater, and when he looked up the German officer had again levelled the pistol and was about to take David's life when an artillery shell landed just beyond the trench, sending up a rain of limbs and earth and David himself, who was propelled high and aloft from the trench, his broken body landing against the semi-erect cross, the tangle of barbed wire snaring him and holding him upright and bleeding.

NINE

I T WAS DIFFICULT FOR DUNNE TO SEE—his vision
was blurred by rain, mist, gunpowder smoke,
and the sides of the sandbags through which he
was looking. His eyes scanned no man's land.

"I don't ..."

"Two o'clock," Godin said grimly.

Dunne stared in that direction, and slowly the
elements of the scene came into focus: fallen bodies, mud, fragmented farm equipment, a shell crater, the distant bags of the enemy's line. Then he
saw him, enshrouded by vapour, affixed to a cross,
his lower body soaked in blood: David.

"Shit," he said, and he continued peering over the field though the sight of it hurt his eyes and made his heart thrum. Even from this distance, he could see that David was bleeding not only from a wound in his thigh but from a dozen different places where the wire holding him in place cut his skin.

"It's him?" asked Godin.

"It is."

Highway scrambled over to Dunne. "What do we do?"

"We get him."

"Soon as any of us goes over the top the enemy'll open fire. We'd be sitting ducks."

"We can't leave him up there."

"We can't get to him either."

Dunne said nothing. His mind whirled.

"Maybe we can wait until dark," Highway suggested. "If he can hold out till dark maybe we'd have a chance."

"He's wounded," said Dunne. "Bad."

"Still."

"He could bleed to death out there. There're three of us dead already and that's enough."

Highway's voice was insistent now. "There'll be *five* if you do what I think you're gonna do."

Dunne felt a calm spread over him: it warmed his fingers, it slowed his heart, it stilled his mind. He was damned no matter what he did, and this was a circumstance that he knew well and understood and felt at home with. Again he looked out over no man's land. He studied the enemy's garrison for minutes and minutes. He then studied the stretch of field separating his position and David's: there was an overturned supply wagon and another shell hole and then there was the enemy. He stretched his neck and looked above him and saw something and was possessed by an idea that felt so fateful and right it disturbed him. For some reason, he thought of Sarah and he thought of that German kid he'd stabbed and he felt his calm turn to something riddled with excitement and dread and an ingrained mistrust of God. His heart sped and his mouth went dry for he knew what was going to happen.

Everything had turned quiet and still and he did not have to yell to be heard.

"Look up," he said.

Godin, Witchell and Johnson did what they were told. Highway did so as well, though he did so slowly to show his disgust.

"You see that huge black cloud rolling in?"

"The one's way blacker than the others?" asked Witchell.

"That one. When it gets here things are gonna darken and it's gonna rain like a son of a bitch and that's when I'm going."

"You'll get killed," said Highway.

"No," said Dunne. "Over on the north side of the Hun line you can see where they've built it up to hide a gunner. Just before I go over everybody's gonna start firing like hell at that spot and the enemy'll think we're going for that gunner and if all goes right I'll get to the kid and get him off of that thing and drag him back before they even know what hit 'em. Just keep 'em pinned down and it'll work."

"For fuck's sake," Highway pleaded. "It won't."

"It has to."

"Ah hell, Mikey, it won't."

Dunne ignored Highway and looked around. "Everybody understand?"

They all stared at him dumbly, not believing his plan, for it was suicide and nothing but, and it was at that moment they all realized they were frightened of Dunne and the forces that moved him. The one exception was Johnson, who was still wincing and holding his hand; someone had bandaged it and in places the gauze bloomed scarlet and in others it was oozing something black and viscous and oddly sweet-smelling. Dunne turned to Witchell and Highway.

"You two go up and down the line and let people know what's happening. Godin, you stay here and man that Lewis gun. You understand?"

"Yeah," they said, though in their voices were notes of dejection and sickness.

"Then go."

The pair scampered along mud and water and running blood and the backs of dead face-down soldiers while Highway and Johnson stayed put, both looking disgusted and sorry. The word travelled up and down the line in garbled half-whispers and then everybody settled and looked upward, like turkeys caught in a rainstorm. It was misting out already, and Dunne thought that the moisture settling on his features felt clean and fresh and good. He waited. There were winds that day, and though they were blowing in the direction of the battlefield they were now slight and meandering. The cloud slowly approached, though there was a period in which Dunne thought it might turn wispy and deteriorate altogether; instead, it seemed to revolve in the air and somehow turn denser and blacker than before. He could hear far-off thunder, rumbling like a large man's cough. He made sure he had a first-aid kit and water and rations clipped to his ammunition belt. He was ready and every nerve was firing. Still, the pitch-black cloud lolled and rolled and revealed a thousand variations in hue, shape and texture.

The rain arrived before the cloud did, the mist turning to heavy cold drops the size of honeybees.

He could hear it tapping against his helmet and the wood of the parapets and the quagmire at his feet. Whatever chatter down the line stopped, for they all knew this rain signalled that the time was close.

The grey enfolding the trench deepened and turned lightless.

"Fire!" Dunne yelled, and then every machine gun and cannon and rifle opened fire on the Fritz gunner site at the north end of the enemy's trench. Dunne rolled over the lip and ran over fallen bodies and scurrying rats and he dove behind the battered wagon. He stayed here for only a second, rain pummelling his back: the enemy was returning fire, though it was clear they were shooting out across the field at the Lewis gunners and so Dunne was again on his feet and he had just about made it to the second shell crater when a bullet ripped into his side and the whole right half of his body bloomed scarlet; pain knifed through all parts of him and then he was spinning and falling next to a cold bloated corpse who had died on his back with his eyes open as though in contemplation of things heavenly. Dunne took several painful breaths and with a scream was up and running, now in a mad frantic racing zigzag, and as he ran bullets shot up geysers of runny black earth all around him, and the only reason he wasn't shot again was a combination of luck and fate and return fire. Ten yards from David he slid face-down in mud to reach the boy, and when he lifted his head he heard someone yelling in German; Dunne looked up and saw that they had pulled their rifles back over the edge of the sandbags and he could also see that they were all looking at him, through gaps in the sandbag wall. The fire from his own trench now ceased and all went silent; he could hear nothing but wind and the Germans chuckling and his own hard-panting breath.

"I'm here, kid," he grunted, though David was shaking and clearly in shock.

Dunne began working at the wire digging into David's arms and legs, but without pliers he accomplished little more than cutting himself. He took a deep breath and felt pain ricochet through him. Even as he worked away, the mud anchoring the makeshift cross was loosening and Dunne realized that the whole thing was going to fall and when it did it fell toward him. Dunne caught it, and as he supported David he knew what was going to happen. He would drag David and the cross through a hundred yards of no man's land and at some point the Germans would tire of this game and open fire and that was the only option available to him and so that was what he accepted he had to do.

Dunne turned beneath the cross so that it

was supported on his back, the Hun feting this manoeuvre with taunts, applause and whistles. On top of him, David moaned and talked nonsense through clacking teeth. He staggered back toward his trench. With his first step, his foot sank into mud and he fell with David on his back, his face falling into mud, and when he rose shakily to his feet he still heard laughter coming from the German trench. He fell again and there came a burst of pain so intense he wondered if something inside him had broken. He kept on. He took step after step and by the time he reached the outskirts of the first crater, he could hear the men from his side starting to urge him on: "Come on, Mikey, you can do it, Mikey," though he wished they wouldn't for he knew this would anger the Germans, who had gone quiet and, Dunne knew, would decide the game was over at any moment and start firing.

"Stop it," he mumbled to his men as he took another slow step. "Stop it, stop it stop it," though it wasn't long before the pain thrumming through his body interfered with his thoughts, and he forgot why he was saying these words—*stop it stop it stop it*—though he kept saying them anyway, for his movements were now intertwined with the two syllables, *stop* ... step ... *it* ... step ... *stop* ... step ... *it* ... step, and after a while it occurred to him that the mumbling of these two words was the only thing keeping him on his feet.

The enemy started firing. Dunne felt something stinging and hot enter his right leg just above the ankle and he fell face-first again into mud. He rolled beneath the cross just as his men opened fire, keeping the Germans pinned beneath their sandbags, though of course this didn't work completely and there were bullets flying over Dunne's head and he knew, again, that his plan had failed. Beside him was the old cart and he watched through deadened blank eyes as it exploded next to him.

Dunne looped his arms over the horizontal plank of the cross and, his back pressed into mud, dug in his boots and straightened his legs, moving David and the cross just a little over the muddy and corpse-strewn field. He dug in his feet again and pushed once more with his legs. This moved them about a yard and he dug his boots into mud and straightened his legs and this moved them another few feet, Dunne groaning with pain and David coming awake and yelling, "Leave me, for fuck's sake, leave me!" The sergeant dug in his feet three more times, and three more times they moved a little farther. Though it was slow going and difficult, it meant that they stayed more or less flat against the ground and were a difficult target. At one point he sat up, just a little, to strengthen his grip on the cross, and a bullet clipped his shoulder and this time his body was so riddled with pain and exhaustion it didn't even hurt, it was as though something soft and windlike had torn open his shoulder. He did notice, however, that his whole right arm didn't work quite as well, and that he could smell something that reminded him of burning fat, so he decided that he'd had enough, that he'd played enough of this German game, that he'd lie back and let it happen, though when he did he saw a kestrel fly overhead and there was something in the hopefulness of the bird's flight that made him continue amid the firing and the yelling and the spewing of his own hot red flowing essence.

Boots in, straighten. Boots in, straighten. Boots in, straighten. His progress was slow and torturous and bullets kicked up little geysers of mud all around. Occasionally, he'd yell, "Stay flat stay flat," though even as he did he noticed he was weakening and growing light-headed. As Dunne dragged David through the mud, he found himself in other places, back in Alberta, riding through mountains; though after a few moments he would find himself back in the war, dragging a kid through mud in a field swarming with fire. When yet another bullet hit him in the upper left arm he thought it was a horsefly bite because he was in a different time and place and having a swim in a waterhole they used to go to as kids. He blinked his eyes and then he was back in Belgium, outside the town of Passchendaele, and he was planting his boots, and he was pushing against mud, and he was planting his boots, and he was pushing against mud, the ground cold and sloppy on his back, the kid helping as best he was able by wiggling free of the wire and pushing with his own feet, though with his mangled leg he howled and screamed and still more fire came, kicking up divots of black bloody mud to the left and to the right of them.

Dig in, straighten his legs, dig in, straighten his legs, and then he could hear his old friend Highway yelling, "Just a little farther! Just a little bit fuckin' farther!" and he knew he was close, and he knew he was still in the middle of battle trying to get this young kid to the trench so he dug his boots in, and he straightened, and he dug his boots in, and he straightened, and he was about to dig in one more time when four pairs of hands reached from nowhere and pulled and he felt a pain more excruciating than any he'd ever known and then he was at a rodeo, roping steer to the roar of a crowd, and there was a girl in the audience, seventeen if she was a day, and she was watching him in that way that meant she'd be loitering near the busters' tent after the show, and that she'd want an autograph and maybe more, and when he awakened it was just a few seconds later, and Highway was over him, fumbling with a first-aid kit and trying to dab at Dunne's wounds with gauze while saying, "We did it, Mikey, we did it. Reinforcements are here. We held the trench, Mikey," and this was so funny to Dunne that he smiled, warm onyx juice spilling from the corners of his mouth. He closed his eyes, and there was a white stallion in the middle of a battlefield, snorting and pawing the ground. He was a beautiful creature, and Dunne wondered why he would be here, in Belgium, near the village of Passchendaele, and when he next opened his eyes he saw the kid, Sarah's brother, freed from the cross and sitting next to the mud trench wall and he was screaming as they tried to treat his leg and his cuts and because he was screaming so loudly Dunne knew that the kid would be all right.

Two stretcher bearers came. He knew this was happening. They put him on a stretcher and then he was being carried through mud and through forest and then he was on horseback, how he'd always loved horses, and as he galloped through forest on the white stallion he saw that the woods were full of those small hawks they called kestrels, and that they were swooping and darting between the branches. They were out of the forest now. He was back on the stretcher and beneath him he heard feet sticking in mud and he felt the jiggle of the stretcher though there was no pain, not here, not in this midway place, and then they pushed through the door of the clearing station and someone yelled, "Nurse!" and there she was, Sarah, leaning over him, crying. He closed his eyes and he was riding the stallion through the mountains. He opened his eyes and he was in the tent and she was still there, weeping, and to stop her from crying he croaked, "David's okay."

"Look at you," she wailed.

"Yeah, all … broken up."

"Oh Michael, you forgot the rule."

He blinked and he was in a warm kitchen, awaiting a meal, and then he was back in the tent during wartime, looking at the woman he loved, and each word caused him a lifetime of pain, but still, still, he wanted to tell her it was okay.

He was in one place only now.

"There's a river outside, Sarah."

"Oh God!" he heard her yelling. "We're losing him!"

"Sarah," he said weakly, "there's a river …"

He even tried to lift a hand to touch her, to let her know it was okay, that they were just sitting down for supper and David and Cassie were coming as well and that it was warm where they were, and the homestead was just how Dunne remembered it as a child, and yet for some reason Sarah was holding him

283

and crying, "Oh Michael, oh Michael, you promised," and he really could not understand why she was so upset, they were having chicken stew tonight with dumplings and corn and bottles of beer, and she was there too, of course she was, he wanted to tell her this for in his confusion there were *two* Sarahs, the one in the kitchen and the one weeping over him, and he liked the one in the kitchen better—it was warm there, it was happy there—so that was where he went, he was sitting at a table with a bowl of steaming hot delicious food in front of him and then he took his first bite and he noticed that that German kid he'd killed for no reason at all was there as well. Not only that, Dunne's parents were there, both of them—when was the last time *that* happened?—and they were happy and alive and Dunne told them he wished they were like that more often. Highway was there too (though he was behaving strangely, he was dressed in battle garb and he was yelling, "Mikey, Mikey, goddamn it, come back!" so Dunne decided to ignore him until he started behaving himself), and Royster was there (how Dunne loved his burly old friend), and even that old drinking buddy who helped him rob a bank, he was there as well and they shared a laugh or two over *that* one. There were children there, little tow-haired creatures that belonged to Sarah and himself, or so he imagined, and suddenly he felt tired, so tired, perhaps he'd eaten too much stew (how he'd always wanted children!), so Sarah came to him and helped him up and took him to a sofa in the other room and he lay on it, amazed by the way in which this day was like every other day, and that every day had led to this day, the last of his life, they were celebrating his ceasing to be, he knew this and was happy about it, it was such a fine way to send a man off, and then Sarah bent over and kissed him and said, "Oh Michael, oh Michael, you forgot the rule," at which point he smiled and closed his eyes and it was at this exact moment that the last spark of will or understanding left Michael Dunne's body and he died.

NOVEMBER 11, 1918

DAVID AWOKE IN HIS RESIDENCE ROOM at the university; it was early, and his roommate, another science major, was still asleep and snoring softly. In the soft light of the room, David packed a few things in a rucksack and, once outside, managed to flag a ride with the driver of a brand-new truck who was heading downtown to pick up supplies for the school cafeteria. Once downtown, David walked along the Bow River until his leg ached. He reached Cassie's house shortly after nine in the morning.

He knocked on the front door and was surprised when Cassie's father answered.

"My boy," he said, proffering his hand. "Come in."

"Sir."

"Cassie will be down in a few minutes. Let's you and I catch up, is that all right?"

"Of course," answered David, though in reality he was still uncomfortable around the doctor.

He followed, limping slightly, into the man's office. When Mrs. Chang brought coffee, he asked for his black with a small amount of sugar.

"So," said the doctor. "First things first. How is the leg?"

"It's fine. More or less."

"More or less?"

"Well. In the mornings it can still bother me. Or if I walk on it much."

"Yes, yes. Of course. That's to be expected. It was quite a wound you had. Only natural it might stiffen up in the night. You were lucky to have kept it."

"Oh I know."

"And your studies? How are they going?"

"Fine, sir."

"Still intent on astrophysics?"

"I am. But I have to take two years of general sciences first."

"Ah yes, Cassie told me as much. Well I think it's a fine thing, David, the way you've straightened out your life. And what about your sister?"

"She's working in a retirement home."

"Ah yes. I heard that too. I fear she got a bit of a bad shake here in town. She certainly proved everyone wrong, however. She is still living in the house on Barrow Street?"

"Yes. It's been cleaned up."

"Good, good. I hear it became a little ramshackle following that business with your father."

The doctor looked up and over David's shoulder. His face brightened.

"Ahhh," he said. "*Here* she is."

David turned and saw Cassie standing in the doorway, dressed in a shawl and long dress and looking more lovely than ever. For some reason, this did not please him, or at least did not please him as much as it should have.

David stood and went to give Cassie a quick, chaste kiss.

"So," said the doctor from behind his desk. "I understand you two have quite a day planned."

Cassie beamed and then giggled and when David looked puzzled, she said, "Daddy's got a little surprise for us."

David looked at the doctor and then at Cassie.

"Come," she said, pulling his arm. "*This* way, silly."

She led him out of the doctor's office toward the front door of the house. She opened it and motioned toward a brand-new Model T, idling on the road outside the house. Cassie waved at the driver, a guy with a moustache the size of a squirrel, who responded by sounding the klaxon.

"We couldn't have you two *walking* all the way into the mountains," said Cassie's father. "Wouldn't want that old war wound of yours to act up, eh, David?"

"No, I ..."

"*David*," said Cassie quietly. "Daddy's hired a car to take us."

David turned to shake the doctor's hand. For some reason, he pictured the things he'd seen in Europe—horrible things, things imprinted upon him forever—and he felt the same icy fear that had possessed him every minute he was there come upon him, as it did several times each day, like a recurring illness.

SARAH AWOKE EARLY and got to Dunne's ramshackle homestead by midmorning. She had come there a number of times since returning from overseas, hoping to find memories of him there. She spent the next hour or two cleaning, and laying out lunch on an old picnic table that she positioned in the sun. Though it was early November, and cool, the alternative was to eat inside the cabin, which was gloomy and cold and, no matter how hard she cleaned, bore the scent of wood rot and mould. She'd told everybody to bring either a sweater or jacket.

Shortly after noon, she heard male voices, coming from afar, and a minute later she saw Royster and Highway tromping over the rise. She ran to them and hugged them both.

"I'm so glad you came," she told them.

"I wouldn't have missed it," said Royster, who was carrying a duffel bag.

"Me neither," said Highway.

"Well, don't just stand there," she said. "Come and have a drink."

The two men sat at the picnic table. When she served them some room-temperature tea, they both thanked her, though she knew that they'd rather have something a little stronger.

They chatted and when the conversation turned to Dunne—they both called him Mikey, she noticed—Royster gestured with his lone hand and said, "I'll be frank, Sarah. I miss him like a brother."

"I know," said Sarah.

"Me too," Highway added. "He *was* my brother."

Suddenly, she felt unaccountably sad. She had no definable way to miss Michael Dunne, yet she did, with a longing that lay deep within her. As Royster and Highway began chatting about something that was happening in the mill, Sarah couldn't help but think of the way she'd been when she'd first met the sergeant. Sad, alone, devoted to hospital tablets. He'd given her her life back, that much was true, and yet she knew that, thanks to him, her life would always include a certain amount of sorrow. (Her only hope was that, with time, her grief would settle and diminish and never go away entirely.) It was the same, in a way, with David: yes, he was a different man now. She could see it in his purposefulness, in his new-found maturity, in the forthright way he carried himself. Yet the jubilance that had once characterized him? It had vanished, perhaps forever, and this, too, was largely thanks to Dunne.

So there it was. She missed him as the sort of person who saved your life but at the same time left your life diminished.

From far off she heard the sounding of a car horn. The three of them stood and went to the edge of the wildflower field and looked down the long, sloping hill separating the homestead from the narrow logging road leading into the mountains. Cassie was helping David out of a brand-new car; Royster and Highway whooped and laughed and yelled jokes about David's coming up in the world. He looked up and waved and, for a single moment, Sarah felt happy.

This, she thought, was enough. This whole day will be worth it, if only for this moment.

THEY ATE ROAST CHICKEN and salad and cornmeal rolls and a peach pie that Sarah had spent the better part of yesterday morning preparing. Beside them, on a patch of thistle and grass and small purple clover, lay Royster's bag, the contents of which were known to everybody, and were the reason for them all being there. There was a distinct chill in the air, though they were high enough in the mountains that the sun was brilliant and warming; only Cassie complained of being a little cold, spurring Highway to pull off his jacket and drape it around the girl's shoulders. Seeing Cassie's expression, Sarah had to stifle a smile. Highway's jacket smelled heavily of tobacco and wood chips and diesel fuel and burnt corn and damp wool, and though Cassie seemed to appreciate its warmth, she wrinkled her nose even as she thanked him.

"Not at all!" Highway laughed, and it was true that he didn't look at all cold, even though his ruddy arms were now bare.

And *yes*, despite her best intentions, a bottle of whisky did eventually appear, courtesy not of Highway or Royster but of David, who had pulled it from his knapsack. Teacups were emptied and then refilled and they toasted the day and the picnic and the coming of peace and when Cassie cheerfully said, "And to fallen comrades!" the rest of them fell silent.

"I'm sorry," Cassie said. "I wasn't thinking ..."

"No, no," said Sarah. "There's no reason to be sorry."

There was a long awkward silence.

"Should we do this?" asked Royster.

"Yes," said David. "We should."

Royster stood and grabbed the duffel and placed it on the far end of the picnic table. He opened it and pulled out a hammer, a box of long nails and a piece of wood. There was a deep, unnatural quiet among them that was tinged with sadness but, at the same time, was a well of many other emotions. They all then walked behind the cabin and found the spot where Dunne, three years earlier, had drunk a bottle of whisky and built himself a grave marker.

It was Royster who finally spoke.

"Who wants to …"

"I will," answered David.

David took the hammer and the length of wood and the box of nails and he went to the cross-shaped marker. He kneeled before it, a movement that took a long time. It was just past two o'clock in the afternoon, and already he had done a lot for one day; his leg was issuing pain into his calves and lower back and the pit of his stomach. He noticed that the air was starting to cool, and that as soon as the sun dropped a little bit more, it would be too uncomfortable to remain outside.

He used the claw of the hammer to remove the horizontal strut. He placed it in the earth. He took the new length of wood—which Royster had made himself, clamping the board in a vise designed for just such a purpose—and he hammered it in place. Again, this took a long time, for the nails were many inches in length, and were ordinarily used for fastening railway ties. He stood and backed away and, like the others, looked at the marker in silence. It now read: *Michael Dunne, 1880–1918.*

He had been thirty-eight years of age when he died, Sarah thought, far older than the vast majority of men who lost their lives in the war. She closed her eyes and thought of the way he had looked when she first saw him; it only took one glance to know that he'd been moulded by forces that were sadder, and different, from those that moulded luckier men. She pictured the lines around his eyes, and she pictured the scars from his cowboy days, and she pictured the way he looked like a completely different person on the rare occasion he smiled. She pictured the way he moved, as though carrying some unseen burden on his back, and she thought of the things he said, things that seemed the opposite of reality until you gave them a moment of thought. Once, in that awful hotel room, weak and crazy from morphine withdrawal, she'd had a moment of lucidity, and she looked over at Dunne and shuddered with embarrassment and said, *I must look awful.* And what did *he* say? What words came out of that tightly held mouth? *Sometimes*, he said, *it's the awful gives us our appeal.*

At the time, she thought he'd said it just to be nice. At the time, she thought he was just being kind. Still, it stayed with her, and it wasn't until much later, with the experience of war behind her, and her being forever flavoured by mourning, that she realized he'd been right.

"Rest in peace, Mikey," said Royster.

These words caused her to weep, and it felt wonderful. Cassie comforted her by putting a hand on her shoulder. For the longest time they stood there, all five of them remembering the sergeant and the war that killed him, until a bank of heavy clouds drifted over the distancing sun and the air turned fragrant and cold and it was time to go home.

PAUL GROSS, known foremost as an actor, is also a writer, producer and director. His portrayal of Constable Benton Fraser on *Due South*, a series he co-wrote and executive produced, received international acclaim. His directorial debut, *Men with Brooms*, broke Canadian box office records. Paul was the recipient of a Golden Nymph Award for best lead actor for his role in H_2O, a Whizbang Films mini-series that he also co-wrote and executive produced. For his portrayal of Geoffrey Tennant in *Slings & Arrows*, Paul was recently awarded his fifth Gemini Award. With *Passchendaele*, Paul fulfills a lifelong dream of bringing this story to the screen and page.